Best ~~BAD~~
BABYSITTERS Ever

PRAISE FOR *BEST BABYSITTERS EVER*

"A clever twist on an old favorite, *Best Babysitters Ever* sparkles with humor and attitude. A must-read for the middle school set!"
—MELISSA DE LA CRUZ, #1 *NEW YORK TIMES* BEST-SELLING AUTHOR

"A glitter-dusted story about ambition, revenge, forgiveness, and friendship. Add to cart!"
—LISI HARRISON, *NEW YORK TIMES* BEST-SELLING AUTHOR OF *THE CLIQUE*

"Hilarious, fresh, and fun! *Best Babysitters Ever* is the best! A great homage to a classic series with plenty of modern moxie."
—MICOL OSTOW, BEST-SELLING AUTHOR OF *MEAN GIRLS: A NOVEL*

"From the start of this debut novel, Cala flexes her prodigious comedic muscles, managing to render the three friends both as sympathetic heroines and as the victims of lives more humorous than they would like. . . . They may never get another babysitting gig, but you're hooked on their story for life."
—*NEW YORK TIMES BOOK REVIEW*

"In her middle grade debut, Cala artfully uses humorous banter to paint the dissimilar friends' realistic relationships as well as their bumbling efforts to vocalize their feelings and advocate for themselves. . . . An appealing, humor-filled update to a classic series." **—*PUBLISHERS WEEKLY***

"Thanks to witty banter, ample humor, and excellent characterization, readers will enjoy following this group of young dreamers as they attempt to gain some independence in their preteen lives." **—*KIRKUS REVIEWS***

"A breezy, entertaining read, this book and the promised sequels seem likely to fill a role similar to the original—as reading material kids choose for themselves." **—*HORN BOOK***

"Fans of the Baby-Sitters Club books are a natural fit for this debut novel about three enterprising girls. . . . Cala incorporates themes of sibling rivalry, jealousy, competition, friendship, manipulation, entrepreneurship, and first crushes into this realistic series starter." **—*BOOKLIST***

"Even readers who have never had the pleasure of hanging out with the BC girls of yore will find Malia, Bree, and Dot all likable in their distinct ways, and they'll appreciate the book's mix of snark and heart." **—*THE BULLETIN***

CAROLINE CALA

Houghton Mifflin Harcourt
BOSTON   NEW YORK

hmhbooks.com

Produced by Alloy Entertainment

alloy**entertainment**

30 Hudson Yards, 22nd Floor
New York, NY 10001
alloyentertainment.com

The text was set in Garamond.
Cover and interior design by Opal Roengchai

The Library of Congress has cataloged the hardcover edition as follows:
Names: Cala, Caroline, author.
Title: Bad babysitters / Caroline Cala.
Description: Boston : Houghton Mifflin Harcourt, [2019] | Summary: Mayhem ensues in their sleepy California beach town when three best friends, motivated by unlimited snacks, no parents, and earning money for an epic seventh-grade party, find an old copy of "The Baby-Sitters Club" and decide to start their own babysitting business.
Identifiers: LCCN 2018021264
Subjects: | CYAC: Babysitters—Fiction. | Clubs—Fiction. | Moneymaking projects—Fiction. | Best friends—Fiction. | Friendship—Fiction. | Humorous stories. | BISAC: JUVENILE FICTION / Social Issues / Friendship. | JUVENILE FICTION / Humorous Stories. | JUVENILE FICTION / Business, Careers, Occupations. | JUVENILE FICTION / Social Issues / Adolescence.
Classification: LCC PZ7.1.C27 Bad 2019 | DDC [Fic]—dc23
LC record available at https://lccn.loc.gov/2018021264

ISBN: 978-1-328-85089-8 paper over board
ISBN: 978-0-358-54765-5 paperback

Manufactured in the United States of America
DOC 10 9 8 7 6 5 4 3 2 1
4500822210

To all the wild girls —
past, present, and future

CHAPTER ONE

MALIA

Technically, the Baby-Sitters Club was someone else's idea. But Malia was the one who stole it, and she thought it was okay to be proud of that.

The epiphany came during the worst week ever. Monday started off with an algebra test where she left half of the answers blank, followed by gym class, where she walked many, MANY semi-aerobic circles around the basketball court, upon which Connor Kelly—aka the only boy worth loving—was practicing free throws. Malia was wearing her new silver leggings and the ultra-curling mascara she'd borrowed from her best friend Bree Robinson even though it made Bree freak out because sharing mascara could apparently lead to eye infections. But Connor didn't look at her once.

On Tuesday morning, Malia walked to school—yes,

walked, on foot like some kind of pilgrim—because her evil big sister, Chelsea, cast her out of their regular carpool. One of Chelsea's dumb friends had a science project that was taking up Malia's usual spot in the back seat, and so she was left without transportation.

Like that wasn't bad enough, on her way down the front walk, she dropped her phone, and the screen shattered into a billion little pieces. Malia could already hear her mom's voice the moment she saw it. *"Ma-li-a,"* she'd say, drawing the name out like some kind of curse word. "You have to learn to be more responsible." Every time she said Malia's name, no matter the occasion, it sounded like it was laced with disappointment. After all, Malia wasn't turning out anything like Malia Obama, the brilliant first daughter after whom she was named. Instead, she was destined to be Malia Twiggs, which anyone had to admit sounded kind of bootleg. This is what led her to rebrand herself as "Alia," a campaign that had been met with moderate success. Malia was still constantly correcting people for including the *M*. But she had faith that eventually it would stick.

It was only October and so far, seventh grade was turning out to be all kinds of meh. Even Malia's once-favorite pastime—killing time at the Playa del Mar Mall—had become insanely depressing. She and her friends wandered in endless loops, eating food-court chicken, and looking at all the things they had no money to buy. Her mom called it "window shopping" and said it was good for building character, but Malia called it "torture," since that's what it actually was.

To make matters worse, seventh grade wasn't bad for everyone. Seemingly all of her classmates were bringing their A game, like Sheila Brown, whose thirteenth birthday party had featured an actual elephant, and Charlotte Price, who'd hosted the most lavish bat mitzvah the world had ever seen. Thanks to her high-flying classmates, Malia's own upcoming birthday was hard to look forward to. Her typical plan—a backyard party with her two best friends—was usually the highlight of her fall, but this year, such a gathering would pale in comparison. Malia had yet to come any closer to realizing how to make her joint-birthday-party dreams a reality.

So anyway, there she was, broke and bad at math, with zero romantic prospects, and now she couldn't even check Instagram without the threat of cutting her fingers. It was almost too much to handle.

"Wisdom of the universe, come to me!" Malia said, which is something her other best friend Dot Marino's mom told her to do whenever she felt confused. Dot's mom was a yogi-slash-tarot-card-reader, which, in their tiny hippie beach town, was actually less weird than it sounds. She was kind of nuts, but in this one instance, Malia figured it couldn't hurt to follow her advice.

Malia continued on her walk for another block, when straight up ahead, she spied a bunch of cardboard boxes outside the local library, labeled *FREE STUFF!* Even she could afford free stuff! It looked like the librarians had gone on a wild cleaning spree, ferreting out any old books, magazines, and DVDs that no longer had a place on the shelves.

The biggest box was overflowing with books — cookbooks, gardening books, an illustrated volume of dog breeds, and a guide to achieving optimum colon health. (Ew.) Malia noticed a little yellow corner peeking out from the middle of the jumble.

She pulled it loose to reveal an ancient paperback. It was wrinkled and worn, and the bottom corner was entirely missing, like someone had tried to eat it and then changed her mind. *The Baby-Sitters Club* was spelled out in red-lettered alphabet blocks, followed by the title *Kristy's Great Idea*. The cover illustration showed four girls wearing the most basic clothes she'd ever seen. Like, there was a turtleneck. And loafers. And a vest. Malia had seen the newer version of this book floating around school, and a couple of her friends had even read it, but the original cover was really something to behold.

Four friends and baby-sitting—what could be more fun? read the tagline. Um, she could think of about eight million things. Still, she couldn't explain why, but she felt like she was meant to find this book. It was a sign from the universe.

Malia settled onto the rickety wooden bench in front of the library and read the first chapter. She learned how Kristy Thomas, a sports-loving tomboy with a mom who said things like "Drat!" had this big idea to form a babysitting club. She and her three friends met multiple times a week, answered a corded telephone, ate various things wrapped in plastic, and got hired to watch people's children. *Weird,* she thought. *Is this seriously what people found fun in the '90s?* The idea of minding kids for money had honestly never occurred to her before. She didn't read much more, but she didn't have to. She had an idea. Technically, she had Kristy's idea. Now it was time to recruit the rest of the club.

CHAPTER TWO

Dot

Jingle-jangle. *Jingle-jangle.*

The first thing Dot saw upon waking was her mother standing over her, waving her hands in sweeping circles just above Dot's body. Her mom's frizzy red hair formed a halo around her face as her long beaded necklaces jangled like wind chimes in the presence of a very powerful ceiling fan. The sleeves of her tunic billowed in the air as she hovered the palms of her hands to rest just above Dot's eyes.

"What. Are. You. Doing?" Dot asked through gritted teeth.

This was not a normal way to wake up. Unless you were Dot. In that case, you were pretty much used to it.

"Dot, honey, there's no reason for an attitude. I was just doing a Reiki attunement."

Dot groaned and pulled her pillow on top of her head. Her

sheets and pillowcases were black—much like the decor in the rest of her bedroom—and thus excellent for blocking out both unwanted sunlight and the antics of eccentric mothers.

"Your energy is feeling a bit orange right now," her mom continued. "Are you stressed about something?"

A perfectly innocent question. Like being jolted awake via crazy witchery was not inherently stressful.

Dot let loose a monotone groan loud enough to drown out whatever statement came next. Dot heard her rummaging around somewhere in the room, no doubt disturbing the highly organized chaos Dot had worked so hard to achieve. Her bedroom was super tiny, so everything—from her expertly styled bookshelves to the painstakingly placed collage that occupied the entire wall above her desk—had its place. She could always tell if anything was moved by even an inch. For a few blissful moments, Dot heard no sounds. Perhaps her mom had vacated the premises. Perhaps she would be permitted to sleep for a few more moments, to escape the heinous reality that was being twelve.

"WHAT is THIS?" her mom yelled.

No such luck.

Dot slowly removed the pillow to discover her mom standing in front of the immaculately color-coded bookshelf, brandishing a stick of deodorant. She waved it in the air like Excalibur, her face filled with a disgust that would be more appropriate had she just unearthed the limp carcass of a recently deceased rodent.

"That is deodorant," Dot said matter-of-factly. After all, she was fairly certain her mom already knew what it was.

"This . . . this . . . chemical cesspool is a known carcinogen!" she spat. "Why is it in our house? What happened to the rock crystal deodorant I bought you?"

"Puberty happened. And then the crystal didn't work anymore." Dot was grateful her mother hadn't yet stumbled across the stash of other contraband products hidden in the closet: lipstick, tinted moisturizer, dry shampoo, and—most controversial of all—spray-on bronzer. Her mom exclusively used natural and organic products, many of which she made herself, like some kind of suburban shaman. She insisted Dot do the same—otherwise risk unimaginable peril—but there was only so much that coconut oil could do. "I mean, the youths of America are out there stealing things and doing drugs. Wouldn't you rather my only vice be proper grooming?"

"NO!" Her mom flung her arms into the air, prompting a whiff of patchouli to waft across the room and assault Dot's nostrils.

Dot staggered out of bed, any hope of a peaceful morning now shattered.

"Mother, maybe you should learn to pick your battles."

"One day you're going to have babies of your own, and then you'll understand," she cried, clutching her hands to her chest. "Unless they come out having three heads because you continue to slather this poison all over your body!"

Dot had often thought her mom missed her calling as an actress. She could easily win an Oscar for her dramatic reactions to all things. Instead, she was a yoga teacher. A very, very theatrical one.

Dot calmly exited the room, though she knew her mom would just follow her around the bungalow. Their home was so freakishly tiny it often felt impossible to get away from her. Dot continued down the narrow hallway, over the layered vintage rugs, past the five-foot-tall amethyst geode, and into the kitchen.

Some kids had parents who made them breakfast, and entire families to eat it with. But her mom had never been much of a cook, and Dot had no siblings to speak of. Ever since her dad left when Dot was little, she'd been expected to rummage through whatever organic, gluten-free goodness they had lying around and fix something for herself. Dot supposed she was thankful for the independence. It would help when she lived on her own one day, far away from the sleepy beach town that was Playa del Mar.

Dot opened the cabinet to survey the goods: hemp flakes (scary); cashew spirulina algae balls (so scary); sugar-free, vegan peanut butter cookies (not quite as scary, but not appropriate for breakfast). She settled on some kind of gluten-free rice flakes that had a picture of a friendly manatee on the box. Why would they use such a benevolent animal to market something so awful?

She poured some flakes into a bowl with the phases of the moon painted along its rim, and drowned the whole thing in cashew milk. They never kept any dairy products in the house, something her mom insisted upon long before it was trendy.

"These flakes taste like nothing," Dot said. "They are truly impressive for how little flavor they possess."

Her mom filled a copper watering can and proceeded to water one of what felt like three thousand ferns dangling from hooks above the counter.

"That's better than if they had a bad taste, no?"

"At least that would provide some sort of experience."

Dot started plotting which snack she'd purchase from the school cafeteria to serve as the second half of her breakfast.

Something completely forbidden, like a huge chewy cookie, made with gluten and sugar and dairy, encrusted with M&M's.

"Just so you know, I'm having my crystal healing group over this afternoon for a full-moon meditation. If you come straight home from school, you're more than welcome to join us. I think Jamie is bringing her Wiccan spear!"

"That sounds, uh, magical," Dot said. "Too bad I'm supposed to meet up with Malia and Bree after school." Her mom's face fell. "But please tell everyone I said hello."

"We'll be sure to do a visualization for you," her mom said. "Is there anything you've been particularly wanting lately?"

Other than the ability to freely purchase the things normal parents kept in the house—like, say, body wash—only one thing came to mind. All Dot wanted was to live in New York City, in an apartment of her own, wearing all-black clothes and talking about interesting things with interesting people—writers, designers, researchers, inventors, entrepreneurs. People who stayed up until the wee hours because they were bursting with ideas and entire worlds they wanted to bring forth. People who wanted to change the world by the sheer will of their passion. The kind of people who just didn't exist in this tiny town. But of course Dot couldn't tell her mother that. That dream was still years away.

In the meantime, though, Dot did have one slightly more practical wish: to throw a birthday party to rival her classmates'.

"Well, Malia and Bree and I are trying to plan our annual joint birthday party..." Dot started, hoping her mom's psychic powers might kick in before she had to straight up ask for a budget. Her mom nodded supportively but said nothing, so Dot was forced to continue. "This year is a big one, since everyone is turning thirteen. Charlotte Price had Drake perform at her bat mitzvah." Her mom showed no sign of knowing who that was. "And Sheila Brown had an actual elephant at her party."

"An elephant! Where on earth did she get an elephant from?" Her mom was indignant. "That's exploitation! Not to mention irresponsible. Did they have a proper handler?"

Dot realized she would have to change her approach. "Of course, we don't want to do anything like that. We love animals! We also love parties. So we're hoping to have a really good one this year."

"I'd be happy to read tarot cards, if you'd like!" said her mom. "Ooh, or I could have my friend Patricia do aura readings."

"Sure!" said Dot, not wanting to hurt her mother's feelings. "I mean, maybe. I'd have to talk about it, you know, with the other girls." She stalled for a moment before continuing. "We were thinking that since this year feels so special, maybe we could do better than the usual bag of chips on a table. Like, maybe we could host it somewhere exciting, at an actual venue."

"A venue?" Her mom wrinkled her nose. This wasn't going the way Dot had hoped. "Why do you girls need a rented space? Filled with the energy of who knows how many people have hosted parties before you."

"We just thought—"

"Dot, my love, I want you to have the best birthday party ever. But I don't think it takes an overpriced location to accomplish that—not to mention all the sugar and artificial coloring and wasteful plastic utensils that often accompany such a bash. Celebrations are about togetherness. You can have that anywhere!"

Dot sighed. This was a lost cause.

"Is there anything else you've been hoping for lately?" her mom asked.

"Well, it might be nice if my armpits could magically stop producing sweat."

"Very funny," her mom said, swooping in for a hug. "I love you, my little Dot."

Legend has it when Dot's mom first saw her on the

sonogram, she said Dot looked like . . . a dot. The name stuck. Dot wasn't sure if her mom had been joking when she told her that story, but Dot didn't care. One day when Dot was famous and important, it would make for a wonderful line in her memoir.

"I love you, too, Mom," she said, and actually meant it. At the end of the day, it was the two of them against the world. As kooky (and messy, and flaky, and eccentric) as she was, her mom was basically everything to her. She worked incredibly hard so the two of them could be comfortable. Plus, she had spawned Dot, after all.

"But I'm keeping this poison death stick!" her mom said, snatching the deodorant off the counter and slipping it into the pocket of her tunic.

Only six more years, Dot reminded herself, as she did each morning. Six more years until she turned eighteen and could live an independent life.

CHAPTER THREE

Bree

S ometimes, when something is so right, you just know. You know?" Bree said.

"Mm-hmm," said her mom, without turning her attention away from the stove.

"And I *know* that if Taylor Swift and I could meet, we would be best friends."

"That sounds great, sweetie," her mom said, placing all her focus on flipping a blueberry pancake.

"What do you think, Taylor?" Bree asked, scooping up their tabby cat and burrowing her face in her soft squash-colored fur. Bree loved the cat so much, almost as much as the real Taylor Swift. She was a really nice cat and probably Bree's favorite family member. She only scratched Bree sometimes.

"No, Taylor! Choc-it Puddin'!" corrected Bree's

two-year-old half sister, Olivia. Their parents had let Olivia name the cat and she chose to call it Chocolate Pudding. But the cat was orange and chocolate pudding is brown, and that name made no sense. So Bree unofficially changed it to Taylor.

Bree's mom loved to remind her that Bree had named their previous pet, a sunfish named Belieber. But Belieber died, along with Bree's love for Bieber the year he got all those tattoos. Plus, everyone knows that naming a cat is a *much* bigger deal than naming a fish. You couldn't even hug a fish.

"Choc-it Puddin'! Choc-it Puddin'!" chanted Olivia, kicking her feet against her booster chair and banging her plastic toddler spoon on the table.

The cat made a perturbed meow and leaped from Bree's arms. Sure enough, it left a scratch. Maybe the cat sensed that no matter what, she would always be second to the real Taylor. Animals were psychic like that.

"What's going on in here?" asked Ariana, sailing into the room in a long, floral dress. It had tiny spaghetti straps and fell almost all the way to the floor. The sheer fabric shifted in the breeze as she walked.

Ariana was seventeen and a senior in high school. She was Bree's stepdad Marc's oldest daughter, so she and Bree weren't actually related. Bree often thought if she couldn't grow up to be Taylor Swift, then she would want to be just like Ariana. Sometimes when Ariana went out, Bree stole her clothes and pretended to be her.

"I was just talking about how if Taylor Swift and I were to meet in real life, we would totally hit it off," Bree said.

Ariana rummaged around in the cabinet until she unearthed an energy bar. "Ugh. Thank god, I thought we were out of these!" she said. With that, she pivoted on one sandaled foot and floated out of the room.

"Is that all you're eating for breakfast?" called Bree's mom, but Ariana was already gone.

"So everyone. It's almost my birthday!" Bree announced. "That means we should probably start planning the annual birthday party. Mom, you said we could make it extra special this year, right? Because I'm becoming a teenager."

"Of course," her mom replied absentmindedly.

"Yesssssss, pancakes!" exclaimed Bailey, Bree's nine-year-old brother, who actually bounced into the room. When Bree's hair was a little shorter, people used to mistake them for twins, which was weird because he was three years younger than Bree. And also, because he's a boy.

Her five-year-old half sister, Emma, followed close behind him. She was wearing a long-sleeved T-shirt and matching leggings printed with multi-colored donuts. Her clothes were way cooler than Bree's when she was in kindergarten.

"Charlotte Price had Drake perform at her bat mitzvah. Can you believe that?" Bree said, slightly louder now that all of her little siblings were in the kitchen. Still, zero family members were willing to share whether they did or did not believe it. "I was thinking, maybe Taylor Swift could perform at my birthday party." Silence. "I think she would totally do it, because we are basically the same person." More silence. "Does anyone want to hear why Taylor Swift and I would definitely be best friends?" Bree asked. Again, no one answered—Emma began counting by twos, Bailey drummed on the table, and Olivia continued to contribute absolutely nothing useful—but no one objected, either, so Bree just kept talking. "Reason one: cats. We both love cats. And Taylor the person would probably love to meet Taylor the cat."

"PUDDIN'-PUDDIN'-PUDDIN'-PUDDIN'!" Olivia shouted.

"Reason two: we both love to be on stage. Taylor's favorite things are obviously music and singing and dancing and performing and I love those things, too."

"Everybody," said Emma, "I can sing all fifty states in alphabetical order. Ready?"

Their mom came to the table with a stack of pancakes and deposited one on each of the plates in front of Bree, Bailey, Emma, and Olivia. Bailey immediately covered his entire plate with syrup, while Olivia hacked her pancake to bits with her spoon.

"Alabama, Alaska, Arizona, Arkansas. California, Colorado, Connecticut!" sang Emma, spreading her arms wide like an opera singer.

"Reason three!" Bree was talking even louder now so everyone could hear her over Emma. "Well, this might be kind of embarrassing, but you know how Taylor has had a lot of boyfriends? Well, I've liked a *ton* of different boys this year. I mean, I guess none of them have really technically been my boyfriend or anything, but I think Taylor and I both have really high standards and it can be super hard to find somebody who's totally worthy, you know?"

A blueberry sailed out of nowhere and hit Bree in the face. Olivia giggled.

"Bree, my love, don't throw food," chided her mom.

"But I—" Bree started.

"Is everyone's lunch packed?" her mom asked.

"I didn't throw—" she tried again.

"The lunches are all lined up by the door already!" said

her stepdad, zooming into, and immediately out of, the room. Marc was wearing his usual uniform of an expensive lawyerly suit, his short brown hair brushed neatly to one side. Though he spent most of his days in an office, Marc was always tan from a regular routine of weekend surfing, and left a trail of cologne in his wake. He wore so much of it, in fact, that when the tooth fairy left money under any of their pillows, the bills reeked of Marc's cologne.

"Mom, Olivia threw it," Bree said loudly.

"CHOC-IT CHOC-IT PUDDDDIIIIIINNNNN'!!!!!"

"What's that, Olivia?" Mom scooped Olivia up and kissed the top of her head. "Yes, you named the cat! You picked such a good name!"

Sometimes Bree secretly wished they could trade Olivia for another cat. They could even name the new cat Olivia. Bree wouldn't mind.

"Oklahoma, Oregon, Pennsylvania, Rhode Island!" sang Emma, putting on her emoji-print backpack and skipping away.

"Dishes in the sink, please!" Mom trilled. She probably said this more than any other phrase, except maybe "indoor voices" and "no curse words" and "no shoes on the carpet" and "don't stick things in Olivia's nose." Okay, on second thought, Bree supposed her mom actually had a lot of phrases.

"But anyway. The thing is, like, I know how silly it probably sounds, because Taylor and I haven't actually met yet, but I'm telling you. I have a *feeling.*"

"Uh-oh. Is it a tingly feeling? Better get that checked out," said Bailey, breezing out of the room.

"What does that even mean?" Bree asked.

But nobody answered. Because everyone had already left.

"It's okay," Bree said to herself, which is something she did when everyone else in her family was too busy to talk to her. "You'll be at school soon and your friends will pay attention to you." And just like that, she felt super excited for the day ahead.

CHAPTER FOUR

~~M~~ALIA

All day, Malia couldn't wait for school to be over. Not just because it was a Tuesday, which always felt like the dumbest day of the week, but because she couldn't wait to tell her friends about the Baby-Sitters Club. Who would have guessed she could feel such passion for an old, mildly stinky paperback about the joys of wearing sweaters and minding children?

First, though, she'd have to endure the dreaded trip home. The minute Malia was released from environmental science, her final class of the day, she sprinted out the middle school's front doors, across the soccer field, and over to the high school parking lot, her denim backpack bouncing forcefully against her body. Malia's sister, Chelsea, was both punctual and impatient, and always insisted on leaving *before* the school buses had a chance to populate the roads.

Malia arrived at Chelsea's green Mini Cooper just in time. The taillights were on, but she hadn't yet pulled out of her parking spot. Malia angrily knocked on the passenger window. Chelsea rolled her eyes, then unlocked the door.

"Were you going to leave without me?" Malia asked, exasperated.

Chelsea just shrugged, as if stranding one's little sister at school was par for the course. Which, in their family, she supposed it was.

Usually, Chelsea's friend Camilla occupied the passenger seat, and Malia would be relegated to ride in the back, alongside the book bags, gym clothes, and discarded sporting equipment. But today, the front seat was empty, so Malia hopped right in.

"Where's Camilla?" Malia asked.

"She got a ride home with her new boyfriend," said Chelsea, expertly backing out of the parking space. "She's been spending, like, a hundred percent of her time with him these days. Because she's lost sight of her priorities."

"Her priorities?" Malia asked.

"School. Sports. Friends. SATs. Volunteering. Getting everything in order for college applications."

Malia had only been in her sister's presence for forty-five seconds and already she felt stressed.

"Some people are perfectly happy being average," Malia said. "Some people prefer to, like, actually enjoy their lives." She originally meant to imply that Camilla was average, but as soon as the words were out of her mouth, Malia realized she was talking about herself.

Chelsea took one perfectly manicured hand off the steering wheel and flipped her long brown hair over her shoulder. She smelled like light, flowery perfume and smug overachievement. Sometimes, Malia fantasized about cutting all of Chelsea's hair off while she was sleeping.

"You lack so much context, Malia. One day you'll see."

"Alia," Malia corrected.

"Malia, discarding a consonant isn't going to change who you are."

"I never *said* I was changing who I *am!* I just prefer it. Why can't you take me seriously?" she snapped.

The car slowed to a stop as they approached a blinking construction sign.

"Huh." Chelsea screwed up her face in a look of confusion.

"It looks like Albatross Avenue is closed. Can you map something for me on your phone?"

"I can't—the screen is broken."

Chelsea let out a low whistle. "Mom is going to kill you."

"I'm aware of that, thanks for the reminder."

"Isn't this, like, the fourth phone you've broken this year?"

"It's the second," Malia corrected.

"Not including the time you spilled juice all over Mom's laptop."

"Yeah . . ."

"And that time you somehow managed to break the whiteboard at school," she added.

"Oh my god, Chelsea, what is your problem?"

"I don't have a problem," she said, her tone more like a parent than a sister who was relatively close in age. "I'm just saying, I understand why mom won't let you have nice things when you clearly don't appreciate their value. There's no way she's going to get you another phone." They drove in tense silence for what felt like a million blocks as Chelsea navigated her way through neighborhood streets, accommodating the detour. Finally, she slowed the car down as they made the turn onto Poplar Place.

"Do you think I'll be voted homecoming queen?" she asked for what must have been the thirtieth time that week.

"*Of course,*" Malia reassured her sister, in a tone she hoped sounded more sincere than jealous. Malia actually did hope Chelsea got it, mainly so she would shut up about it.

As soon as the car pulled into their driveway, Malia bolted out the passenger door and down the sidewalk. She couldn't get away from Chelsea—and back into the company of normal humans—soon enough. It was hard enough making it through her days without failing every test or breaking everything in sight. Chelsea's presence only served to hammer home Malia's inferiority. Luckily, Malia saw Dot and Bree already sitting at their regular spot, the little gray gazebo at the end of the cul-de-sac.

Dot and Malia had been best friends ever since Miss Kogan's kindergarten class. With her long honey-colored hair and lightly freckled face, Dot was ridiculously—almost unintentionally—pretty. And with her extensive knowledge of random vintage pop culture—like John Hughes movies and obscure '90s bands—she was chock-full of trivia that boys found charming. She always had an argument ready for anything. Other people could find Dot intimidating, but once you got to know her, it was impossible not to love her.

Bree moved here when they were in first grade, after her mom remarried and they bought the biggest house on Poplar Place. She and Malia immediately bonded over the fact that none of the crayons in art class effectively matched either of their skin tones (Malia's was brown, while Bree's was what her mother confusingly deemed "olive"). They also bonded over eating glue, which was obviously Bree's idea. Later that year, the school replaced all the crayons to better reflect the diversity of the student body, but their friendship was already cemented.

As Malia walked toward the gazebo, she saw they were engrossed in something on Bree's phone. When she got closer, she realized they were watching a YouTube video of Sheila Brown's party from the previous weekend. Even Dot, who said such a celebration was "bourgeoisie" and "contrived," had seemed mildly enthusiastic while perched atop the elephant's big gray body.

"You guys!" Malia exclaimed, pulling the book from her bag. "I have. The answer. To all. Our problems."

No one looked up.

"GUYS! Connor Kelly just said he loved me on social media!" That got their attention. "Just kidding! But I have something to show you." Malia held the ratty paperback aloft, like it was Simba from *The Lion King*. A duo of confused expressions stared back at her.

"I think Ariana used to have that book!" said Bree. "Although it probably got sacrificed in my mom's insane cleaning spree. A couple months ago, she kept running around the house muttering 'Marie Kondo!' and putting everyone's stuff into garbage bags."

"Wait, what? Who's Marie Kondo?" Malia asked.

"Some crazy lady who wrote a book about how tidying is magic," Bree explained. "Anyway, we gave away, like, every single thing in the house."

"You shouldn't let your mom just give things away. Ariana's really stylish," said Dot, pushing her giant tortoiseshell glasses farther up the bridge of her nose. "You could have easily sold everything and kept the money."

"YOU GUYS. If you'd listen to me, I have another way to make money. Money we can use for our own incredible party." Finally, the group fell silent. "Okay, so I found this book, about four girls who form a babysitting club. They're all a little different—there's a tomboy and a Goody Two-shoes who wears loafers and a cool girl from New York City—"

"Ooh, can I be like that one?" asked Bree, rocking back

and forth in her seat. The rickety gazebo floorboards groaned a little under the force of her enthusiasm.

"—and one whose parents won't let her wear dangly earrings and eat junk food, but she does that stuff anyway."

"Oh, I love earrings! Maybe I'm more like her," Bree said, tucking her shiny black hair behind her ear.

"You can be whoever you want!" Malia said, exasperated. "The point is, do you know *how* the four girls buy the clothes and the candy and the makeup they wear on actual dates?"

"They make cash money. By babysitting," Dot chimed in. "P.S. I already read all those books like three years ago. A lot of people have."

"That's fine. This isn't about reading the book—I'm not saying we form a book club. I'm saying we form a babysitters club. We can advertise at school and tell everyone we're open for business. Parents call us when they need a sitter, and we make easy money. I can get a new phone, Dot, you can buy all the deodorant and processed food you want, and, Bree, you can . . ." Malia trailed off. Bree's family was loaded, so her situation wasn't quite as dire. But then again, who didn't want their *own* money? "Most importantly, though, we can raise funds for an amazing party on our own."

"But we don't even like kids?" said Bree, though it sounded like more of a question.

"We technically *are* kids. Plus, this sounds like kind of a huge time commitment," said Dot, twirling a piece of golden hair around a metallic-black-painted fingertip. "Also, no one has actual clubs anymore. Social media has made them obsolete."

Malia rolled her eyes. This was harder than she thought.

"All of that may be true. But none of it matters. Think of it like this: we get to hang out, eat other people's snacks, and watch other people's Netflix. We can try on the parents' shoes and use their expensive makeup and hair products when they aren't home. We don't even have to clean up after ourselves! And at the end of it, we get paid. All we have to do is make sure nobody, like, dies."

Slowly, her friends started nodding their heads.

"Plus, just think about it. How nice will it feel to pool some of our earnings and put it toward our joint birthday party?"

Bree's parents usually sprang for some decorations and a cake in the shape of whatever was popular that year, but nothing had ever come close to creating the kind of excitement spawned by a rapper or a circus animal.

"To have any chance of competing, we need to do something major," Malia concluded. "This is the way."

"Well, when you put it that way, it sounds like a no-brainer," said Bree. "I spend most of my time watching kids at home for free. I might as well get paid to do it for other people! Plus, um, I've kind of always wanted to be in a club."

Malia and Bree both stared at Dot, who was pretending to be transfixed by an ant making its way across the floor of the gazebo. Finally, she held up both hands in a sign of surrender. "Fine. I'm in. But I don't change diapers."

"Aw, you guys! This is so fun. How do we do this?" asked Bree, flapping her hands like an excited penguin.

"We should tell our school to post something on their Facebook page so parents know we're in business," Malia said. "If we hate it, we can always stop."

"Sounds fair enough," agreed Dot, crossing her freckly arms. If Malia had Dot's approval, clearly the idea was a winner.

"Also, we should each have a specific job. Like, the Baby-Sitters Club had a president, a secretary, and a treasurer." Malia was proud of herself for being so organized.

"That's . . . quaint," said Dot. "But I believe in thinking

big. We should have a CEO. And a chief operating officer. And a director of marketing."

Malia nodded and tried her best to look convinced. She didn't want to admit that she had absolutely no idea what any of those jobs meant. Luckily, Dot kept rambling.

"Malia, you can be the CEO, which is basically like the president."

"Alia," she corrected her. "Remember? It's Alia now."

Dot rolled her eyes, making absolutely no move to correct herself. "I'm probably the most creative, so I'm happy to head up marketing. I'll come up with our mission statement and build our website. Bree, that means you're in charge of operations. Does that sound okay?"

"What does operations mean?" asked Bree. "We don't, like, do surgery. Do we?"

"I sincerely hope you're kidding," said Dot. Bree didn't let on one way or another. "In our case, operations means you're the one in charge of finding us actual jobs. Like, maybe you can hit up the parents of your little siblings' friends, by getting the contacts off their class email lists."

Malia had to hand it to Dot—she was pretty good at figuring this stuff out.

"Ewwwww!" shrieked Bree, pointing at something in the distance.

Malia turned around expecting to find a tarantula the size of an SUV. Instead she saw three kindergarten boys—Chase, Clark, and Smith—playing by a nearby bush. Malia's parents loved to point out how they all had first names that sounded like last names. Because Malia's parents were so awesome at picking names.

The boys had built a circle out of rocks, with a stick propped up in the middle. Malia watched as one by one, the five-year-olds plunged their fingers deep into their noses, like they were digging to reach a foreign land. When they unearthed a decent enough treasure, they added it to a small, boogery pile at the top of the stick.

Malia stood up and walked a little closer to them. If she was going to babysit, she reasoned, she should probably figure out how to deal with kids. As a younger sibling, it wasn't exactly her strong suit.

"What are you doing, squirts?" Malia asked. The Baby-Sitters' Club founder, Kristy Thomas, called her little brother squirt, and it seemed like a nice vintage thing to say.

Smith looked up at her. "We're making a sacrifice to the

squirrel gods," he said, like this was a completely normal endeavor. Then he turned back to the crew and plunged his pointer finger into his left nostril.

"YOU WOULDN'T UNDERSTAND! YOU'RE A GIRL!" Clark added, with a very unnecessary amount of rage.

Ugh. Children were weird AND gross. Yet here Malia was encouraging her friends to spend time with them. On purpose. She made a mental note to negotiate rates that were worth it.

Then again, everyone was a little gross. That was part of being a person. As usual, it made Malia think of Connor Kelly, who was about as perfect of a human specimen as one could find. Even he had his moments. The other day at lunch, he was eating a burrito when he laughed so hard he snorted a black bean out of his nose. It shot all the way across the table and hit Aidan Morrison in the eye. It should have been gross, Malia thought, but it wasn't. It was cute.

Malia turned back to her friends, who were smiling and laughing. They'd already moved on from the booger incident, and were casually stalking someone's whereabouts on Instagram.

Everything was going to be great.

What could possibly go wrong?

CHAPTER FIVE

Dot

Dot wasn't entirely sure how to feel about this whole Baby-Sitters Club thing. Yes, she was drawn to the promise of a regular income. She wanted an amazing party just as much as her friends, and that was only the beginning. She'd already made a mental list of things she'd buy once they were in business, and it was not short. She could practically taste the limited-edition seasonal Oreos and smell the clouds of dry shampoo waiting in her future.

But in the present, she felt anxious. No amount of money could change the fact that children were horrid. Starting a business was a lot of work. And despite the part where she had a pretty decent grasp of what makes people tick, she'd never actually held a marketing job before. Or any job, for that matter.

"Our growing organization is stressing me out," Dot

announced as soon as Malia and Bree had settled in her bedroom for their first official club meeting. Malia sat backward on Dot's desk chair, while Bree sprawled out on her stomach across the bed. Dot nervously paced back and forth between them. "We have a lot of stuff to do if we're going to get this business off the ground."

"Way to be a killjoy," said Malia.

"To get things rolling, I have a couple ideas for the website," Dot said. "I think it might be cool if we populate it with stills of babysitters from old movies, like from way back in the eighties and nineties, when it was cool for teenagers to babysit."

"Parents will probably love that, because they're old," added Malia.

"Yes, I think it will totally resonate." Dot nodded.

Bree screwed up her face. "Huh?"

"You know, resonate — when an idea stirs up feelings in somebody. Like, if Malia were to hear a pop song about unrequited love. That would *resonate* with her, because she loves Connor Kelly but he doesn't care about her."

Malia shot her a death stare. "It's Alia. Who Connor *could* have a secret crush on. And Alia would like to go back to talking about the website, please."

"Right, yes," Dot continued. "So the site could also have an 'about' section, with a photo of us and a little bit of background about our unique skills."

"You guys, this sounds so nice!" said Bree. "I'm so excited!"

"We also need to develop a system to track our progress," Dot continued. "I think we'll feel more motivated to hang out with nasty children if we can see at a glance how much money we're actually earning. We can make an Excel spreadsheet—"

"Or a poster!" said Malia, like this was art class.

"Ooh, yes, a poster! With a picture of Taylor Swift on it!" Bree clapped her hands. "Or it can be a collage with, like, lots of pictures of Taylor Swift. I have a box in my room filled with photos of her that I cut out of magazines. There are probably four hundred in there, at least."

"Let's keep our eyes on the prize," Dot said. "Our goal is to throw the most amazing party this town has ever seen—not to mention other stuff, like success and freedom and red-velvet Oreos. We already know what Taylor Swift looks like."

"Yes, but what could be more inspirational?" Bree asked.

"A party," said Malia.

"Oh, right," said Bree.

"Let's not limit ourselves," Dot said, pacing back and forth in front of her color-coded bookshelf, her wall full of vintage concert posters, and her collection of old records. "My financial goals are varied and far-reaching. Clothes. Candy. Deodorant. Eventually, New York. The sky's the limit."

"Speaking of far-reaching, I got access to the elementary school listserve," said Bree. "It's actually really easy, so we can send out our first email blast, if you want."

"Oh my god, it's like our debut!" Malia nervously tapped her pen against the desk.

Dot flinched. It could be an only child thing, or a by-product of the nosy-mom-who-searches-through-her-stuff thing, but it bothered Dot whenever anyone was all up in her personal space the way her friends were right now. They inevitably touched things and moved them around and made scratches on surfaces where no scratches were before.

"Um, Alia? The pen. Could you not?" Dot figured if she used her new made-up name, maybe Malia would be more receptive. It worked; Malia ceased her tapping.

All things considered, though, the e-blast was a cinch to put together. The girls just filled out their names and contact information (Malia insisted on using her recently fixed phone so she could feel "presidential") and a short description of the service they provided ("swift, responsible babysitting by a team of experienced professionals"). Then the server blasted it out to all the parents with kids in kindergarten through fourth grade.

So what if they lied about the part where they had experience? After all, they'd *been* small children not long ago. Shouldn't that count for something?

"Woo-hoo!" said Bree, snapping Dot's laptop shut.

They high-fived one another. Then they stared at the phone, waiting for their first call to come in. Another minute ticked by. Nothing happened.

"Is the ringer on?" Bree asked.

"Yes," said Malia.

"And the volume's turned up?" Bree asked.

Malia double-checked it. "Yep," she confirmed.

"Hmm," Dot said.

The three of them continued to sit there, gazing at the phone, its silence being mocked by the gentle sitar music drifting in from the living room stereo, where Dot's mom was leading in a guided meditation.

They looked back and forth at one another. Dot could practically hear them blinking.

"Maybe we could go knock on a few doors in the neighborhood," said Malia after ten seemingly endless minutes had ticked by.

"Like Girl Scouts?" Bree asked.

"Like proactive people," Malia said.

"That sounds so fun!" said Bree. "But it makes me wish we were selling Girl Scout cookies. Or maybe just that we were eating Girl Scout cookies."

"Just think of all the cookies we can buy once business is rolling," Dot said.

And so, they decided to take the show on the road.

Dot once read that you only get one chance to make a great first impression. So at her urging, the three of them ran home to change into more appropriate attire before making house calls.

Dot settled on her most professional outfit: black T-shirt, black skinny jeans, black ballet flats. She was going for a kind of Audrey-Hepburn-meets-French-au-pair vibe. She wanted her clothes to say, "I'm responsible enough to watch your children, and also stylish enough to provide sartorial inspiration." If she were a parent, she imagined that's something she'd care about.

"What's with all the black? You look like a mime," said a denim-shorts-clad Malia as they made their way down Poplar Place en route to their first house.

"I'm going to take that as a compliment, thankyouverymuch," Dot said, and then added, "Did you even change? You look like you're heading to or from some nonexistent softball practice."

Bree, on the other hand, was one sparkle shy of a Halloween costume. She glittered all over — sparkly headband, sparkly eye shadow, shimmery leggings, silver sandals, and a huge silver backpack to top it all off. She looked like the human embodiment of a My Little Pony.

"Bree, do you want to, like, borrow a blazer or something?" Dot asked. Then clarified, "You know, so people don't think you're unprofessional."

"Or a professional figure skater," added Malia.

Bree looked confused. "But children love sparkles," she said.

They made their way up to the first home on the block, a pretty two-story white house with navy-blue awnings, owned by the Woo family. Dot pressed the doorbell, then waited. Five seconds, ten seconds, twenty seconds. There was no sign of life.

"Maybe they're not home," she said with a shrug.

They were just about to leave when an exasperated Mrs. Woo flung open the front door. Her hair darted in at least eighteen different directions and there appeared to be flour splattered in artful puffs all over her clothes.

"Good afternoon!" Dot started. "I'm Dot, and this is Malia and Bree, and we've recently formed a new babysitting—"

"Babysitting! Yes! Please come in." Mrs. Woo stepped aside and gestured for the girls to enter. "How much time do you have? I have a bunch of errands I'd love to run, so if you could just hang out for a couple hours, that'd be perfect."

"You want us to babysit . . . right now?" Dot ventured.

"YES!"

Well, this was unexpected.

"You girls are in what grade again?" she asked.

"Seventh," Dot answered, flashing her biggest smile, like she was running for political office.

A little furrow formed between Mrs. Woo's brows. "So you're how old?"

"Twelve. But we always work as a team, to provide maximum supervision."

"Whatever, that sounds great," she said, waving a hand. "Do you have cell phones?"

"Yes," they all said in unison.

"Do you know how to use them?"

They nodded.

As Mrs. Woo surveyed them, Dot realized how little their attire—or credentials—actually mattered. They could have been wearing anything, including matching T-shirts with curse words printed on them, or even no clothes at all. Mrs. Woo seemed so absurdly psyched to be getting out of the house, she barely paid them any attention.

"Wonderful! I'm sure you'll be fine." The three of them exchanged excited glances as Mrs. Woo barreled on. "There is plenty of food in the fridge and cabinets. Help yourselves to whatever you want. All of our emergency contact information is on the fridge. Um, I'll be back by seven."

She grabbed her purse and scooted straight out the door, faster than a flaming hermit crab scuttling back to the sea.

And just like that, they were in business.

CHAPTER SIX

ALIA ALIA ALIA

It started out nicely enough. The Woo girls—Ruby, age five, and Jemima, age three—weren't particularly gross or annoying. The little one, with a ponytail on top of her head that resembled a waterspout, was even sort of cute.

"So, what do you guys want to do?" Dot asked, in a pitch that was slightly higher and more animated than her usual dry monotone. It was then Malia realized that aside from Bree's siblings, she'd never seen Dot attempt to interact with a small child before.

"I want to play chefs!" announced Ruby.

"What does that entail?" Malia asked. Her mind immediately jumped to a kitchen engulfed in flames.

"Mom lets us play it all the time. We put a bunch of stuff in a bowl and then I mix it all up," explained Ruby.

"And then YOU eat it!" added Jemima, clapping her little imp hands.

Dot, Bree, and Malia looked at one another and shared a collective shrug.

"Uh, sure, that sounds great!" Malia said.

"YAYYYYYYYYYY!" yelled Jemima, running toward the kitchen, her ponytail bobbing all the way.

"You guys play chefs. I'm going to take a tour of the rest of the house," said Dot in her regular voice, before she disappeared from sight.

Bree and Malia trailed the girls into the kitchen. Everything in the Woo house was white — white ceramic floor tiles, white carpet in the living room, white furniture as far as the eye could see. The kitchen was no exception. How did they keep it so clean with two little kids running around?

"If you can't stand the heat, get out of the kitchen!" said Ruby, jumping up and down while pulling various items out of the fridge. "Why did the chicken cross the road?" She barely paused before concluding, "Because you didn't cook it!" Both girls dissolved into a fit of giggles.

"Can I play chefs, too?" asked Bree.

"No!" yelled Ruby. "Get out of my kitchen! I'm Gordon Ramsay and your food SUCKS!"

Bree turned to Malia, stricken. *That child is evil!* she mouthed.

The girls continued unloading every imaginable item from the fridge—ketchup, mustard, pickles, sauerkraut, sriracha, maraschino cherries—and lining them up on the counter. Malia surveyed the wide range of smells and colors they had amassed in mere minutes, and imagined them splattered all over the kitchen. "Chefs" suddenly seemed like a very bad idea.

"Hey, guys! How about if we play something else?" Malia ventured.

"NO!" yelled Ruby.

"NO-NO-NO-NO-NO!" parroted Jemima.

"How about hide-and-go-seek?" asked Bree.

The girls stopped grabbing foodstuffs and exchanged mischievous grins.

"We LOVE hiding!" Ruby said, prompting Jemima to giggle.

"Great! We're going to close our eyes and count to thirty," said Bree. "Ready?"

The girls nodded.

"One, two, three, four . . ."

They heard the sound of small feet scampering away. As the footsteps faded off into silence, Bree stopped counting. Malia opened her eyes and gave Bree a defeated shrug before opening the fridge and placing all the condiments back inside.

"I can't believe we're already, like, babysitting," Bree said.

"I know!" Malia laughed. "I thought we would at least have time to research or something."

"How long should we wait before trying to find them?" Bree asked.

"I dunno. Little kids are super bad at hiding," Malia said. "They'll, like, stand in the corner, in plain sight. We might as well wait a few minutes so we can enjoy some peace."

They took this as an opportunity to snoop around the Woos' home. The television was very large. The living room couch was delightfully squishy. The wall leading up the staircase was packed tight with family photos: trips to Disneyland and Hollywood, hiking and beach weekends, dance recitals, baby photos, and costumes of Halloweens past. Bree and Malia took their time looking as they slowly made their way up the staircase.

Dot appeared at the top of the stairs. "Where are the kids?" she asked.

"We're playing hide-and-go-seek!" said Bree.

"Did you hear them come up here?" Malia asked.

Dot shook her head.

"Squirts?" Malia ventured. "Come out, come out wherever you are!"

The three of them slowly made their way through the house, searching everywhere. The girls weren't in their shared bedroom, or their parents' room, or any of the bathrooms. They searched beneath the tables, under beds and couches, inside the closets, even in the oven (Bree's idea). Ruby and Jemima were nowhere to be found.

"Ruby? Jemima?" called Bree.

No answer.

"Guys! No more hiding!" Malia yelled.

"If you come out now, you automatically win!" Dot added.

Nothing. Not even a sound.

"I . . . I don't know what happened," said Bree helplessly. "What if they're really gone?" She looked like she might cry.

"They have to be here somewhere," Dot said, visibly trying to remain calm. "Their legs are less than a foot long. How far could they possibly go?"

"We're willing to declare this a victory!" Malia shouted. "Come out whenever you want!"

Still nothing.

"Should we look in the garage?" Malia suggested. At that point, it was the only place they hadn't searched.

Slowly, they cracked open the hallway door that led to the garage. It was dusty and crowded, with stuff piled floor to ceiling—gardening tools, a lawn mower, the girls' tiny bicycles, boxes of holiday decorations, old bowling trophies, and lord knows what else.

"I don't think we should go out there," Bree said nervously.

"We have to at least look," Malia argued. "They have to be *somewhere*."

Malia bravely—or maybe it was more like dumbly—ventured down the stairs. She had only taken a few steps forward, when, in typical fashion, she tripped on a rake. In her defense, the garage was dimly lit and the tool seriously came out of nowhere. Malia staggered forward, catching her balance before she could fall down. The rake flew a few feet forward, clattering to the ground with a tremendous sound.

Still, there was no sign of the Woo kids anywhere.

After taking one more lap through the house, they headed back to the kitchen, defeated.

"Do you think they actually left?" Bree asked, nervously picking the polish off a fingernail.

"That's against the rules. You can't hide-and-go-seek outside a property's zoning regulations. It's not called hide-and-go-trespass," said Dot, slamming her hands down on the counter.

"What if they ran away from home? What if we go to jail for losing them?" Bree whined.

Dot plunged her head into her hands. "That's the worst story ever. Once upon a time, three girls got hired to babysit. And then they went to jail. The end."

"I'll never meet Taylor Swift from the inside of a prison," Bree whispered as one lone tear trickled down her cheek.

"There's no need to panic. We didn't technically do anything wrong," Malia said, unconvincingly.

Just then, Bree snapped into action. "You guys, it's time to resort to emergency measures." She pivoted with military precision and retrieved her silver backpack from the kitchen floor. She unzipped it, only to unearth the contents of an entire supermarket candy aisle. Bree pulled out bag after bag of candy, in all shapes and sizes: gummy bears, peanut butter cups, mini chocolate bars, sour gummies, chocolate caramel turtles.

"Sugar! You've been holding out on me!" Dot gasped, seeming genuinely miffed.

"What are you doing?" Malia shrieked. "Is this really the best use of our time?"

"This is. The secret. To dealing. With children," Bree said calmly.

"Dude, at the moment, there are. No children. To deal with. The children are *missing*. Like, we are maybe going to get arrested for losing them. And you're setting up a lovely dessert bar? This isn't a bat mitzvah."

Bree continued tearing into each of the bags and depositing their contents into different size bowls. The candies made melodic tinkling sounds as they made their journey into each vessel, like a sweet symphony of sugar. Just then, they heard a sound even sweeter than glucose hitting ceramic: the stampede of miniature feet running their way.

"SUGARRRRRRRRRRR!" yelled Ruby.

"CHOC-CHOC-CHOCKO-CHOCK-CHOCK-LET!" yelled Jemima. Just because she couldn't say "chocolate," it didn't stop her from wanting to inhale it.

Dot and Malia stood there with their mouths hanging open.

"I told you," said Bree.

"What the—" Malia started, at the same time as Dot said, "But you didn't even know we were babysitting today! Why do you have so much stuff?"

"I live with small people. This is how you keep the power."

"Where were you guys?" Dot yelled.

But the girls were too excited to answer. They grabbed tiny fistfuls of candy and shoveled them goblin-style into their mouths. Soon Ruby was whirling in dizzy circles, spinning like a child-shaped top while Jemima hopped all around her, yelling in gibberish, like a demonic rabbit.

They'd just finished stashing the evidence of their candy trickery into Bree's backpack when they heard the scrape of a key in the front door.

"Quick! How do we take the batteries out of these things?" Malia asked, pointing at the deranged kids. Surely, Mrs. Woo would notice that her children were practically vibrating from the sugar.

"MOM'S HOME!" yelled Jemima.

"NOT THE OGRE! NOT THE OGRE! EVERYONE MAN YOUR STATIONS! HEAD FOR THE BRIDGE!" yelled Ruby.

"AAAAHHHHHHHHHH!" Jemima screamed, throwing her hands in the air.

The girls' mother appeared in the kitchen doorway.

"Hi, Mrs. Woo!" Dot trilled, giving her a tiny little wave, like a beauty pageant contestant.

"How were your errands?" added Bree, completely ignoring the bedlam unfolding around them.

Mrs. Woo entered the room slowly and gingerly, like the

lone survivor in a zombie movie, surveying the wreckage of the planet she once called home.

"Oh my," Mrs. Woo said as Jemima ran straight into the wall. The force of it caused the little girl to fall backward and land on her back, her tiny feet kicking upward like an over-turned beetle. "I've never seen them like this before. They're so . . . energized."

Uh-oh.

Ruby pulled Jemima to her feet and the two of them careened toward Malia, wrapping their tiny arms around both of her legs in a surprisingly strong embrace.

"Can they come play again?" Ruby shouted.

"Please, please, PLEASE!" Jemima added.

Mrs. Woo shook her head in disbelief. "Wow, they never like anyone!" Her face broke into a wide smile. "Can you girls possibly come back next weekend? Maybe Sunday afternoon?"

Malia, Dot, and Bree exchanged glances. Had they actually pulled this off? More importantly, could they possibly do it again? What if they really did lose the kids next time? Or worse?

But then something magical happened. Mrs. Woo pulled out her wallet and counted out a stack of crisp twenty-dollar bills.

"Um, YES," they all said in unison. "We can come back Sunday."

"I am SO glad to have found you three!" she said, handing the money to Malia. "This is such a lifesaver." The moment the cash hit her palm, all of Malia's fears evaporated. It didn't matter if kids were even worse than cavities and routine vaccinations and standardized tests *at the same time*. They were a road that led to money.

CHAPTER SEVEN

Bree

After not losing the Woo kids, Bree, Malia, and Dot
made their way back to Malia's house to regroup.
Malia's room was always a disaster, and today was no exception. Clothes, books, magazines, and random sporting goods
were strewn on every surface. Bree pushed aside a math text-
book, crumpled gym clothes, and a yearbook open to Connor
Kelly's photo, to clear some space on the floor.

That's when Malia's phone rang.

"Oh, hiii, Ms. Larsson," said Malia, making eyes at Bree
and Dot and giving them a big thumbs-up. Dina and Erika
Larsson had boy triplets—Thor, Ruckus, and Bronson. They
lived in a giant house overlooking the beach and they were
super nice. Malia switched her phone onto speaker so they
could hear the conversation.

"Cynthia Woo just told me what a tremendous job you all did watching her girls, and I was wondering if I could possibly hire you for later this week?" trilled Ms. Larsson. "We'll be happy to pay a premium, of course, since it's for three children."

The girls' eyes widened when she told them her rates — it was more than twice what Mrs. Woo had paid. If they could babysit regularly, they'd be totally set.

"Erika and I have to go to this fundraiser to benefit the elusive Pacific narwhal," Ms. Larsson continued. "It could run pretty late into the evening, until nine or ten at least, so you'd have to stay past bedtime."

"We'd love to!" the girls all chimed at the same time.

Bree couldn't remember another time she'd ever been more excited, except maybe that one time she won the guess-how-many-jelly-beans-are-in-the-jar contest at school and her prize was ALL OF THE JELLY BEANS (1,378 of them!) and also her birthday the years she turned four, six, seven, nine, ten, and twelve, and also, every single Christmas. Because presents, obvi.

Malia's bedroom door swung open a crack.

"Why were you talking to Dina Larsson?" asked Chelsea, popping her head through the doorframe.

"Why were you lurking outside my room?" Malia spat back.

"Everyone knows the hallway is neutral territory, *Malia*," Chelsea retorted.

"My name is Alia and my personal affairs are none of your business!" Malia yelled, and slammed the door in Chelsea's face.

"You guys! What just happened was an amazing moment," Bree said.

"Ugh, no it wasn't. My sister is the worst," said Malia-Alia.

"No, not that! I meant Dina Larsson calling. It was like an actual moment from the Baby-Sitters Club. We're sitting in our founder's bedroom, when a call comes in, and just like that, we book a job. WE'RE IN BUSINESS!" Bree said, breaking into a dance that she hoped would make Taylor Swift proud.

"You know what? You're right!" said Malia. "I think we deserve to celebrate!"

"I couldn't agree more," added Dot. "And what better way to celebrate than retail therapy?"

The answer was clear. It was time to go to the mall.

Glitter was honestly the best. Bree knew not everyone had an appreciation for it (ah-hem, Dot) but those people probably didn't know how to have fun. And Bree felt bad for them, because fun was so much fun. You know?

Bree wasn't aware of exactly how many types of glitter there were in the universe, but it was really a lot. There was glitter nail polish, obviously, but also glitter eyeliner, glitter sneakers, glitter backpacks, glitter phone cases, glitter pens, glitter sunglasses, glitter bikes with matching glitter helmets . . . Like, picture all the normal things that already exist in the world. Now picture them sparkly. How amazing is that?

Bree knew they were supposed to save for the party, but from the moment Mrs. Woo handed over the money, Bree wanted to buy it all. She wanted every inch of her life to be covered in glitter.

Mall roaming was something they did on the regular, but this time, everything felt different. That mall smell—a mixture of French fries, perfume samples, floor cleaner, and happiness—was more delicious than usual. Everything even looked different: bigger, brighter, bursting with shiny new objects that made Bree's heart hurt from how much she wanted them.

Usually, her mom gave Bree a shopping allowance and told her to have fun, but then she'd want to know what Bree spent it on. With her own money, it was like Bree could do anything she wanted.

"Smart businesses reinvest their money back into the company," said Dot as Bree lovingly petted a denim jacket with sequin patches. "Like taking out ads on social media or making merch for the kids with our logo on it."

"Dude, where do you learn this stuff?" asked Malia.

"What? Who doesn't know that?" Dot asked.

"I love you guys!" Bree said. Because she did love them, and also because she didn't know how else to participate in the conversation.

They rounded the corner, where they spotted a bunch of boys from school hanging out near the surf shop. Boys were so weird, because they went to the mall as much as girls did, but they never bought anything. They just roamed around in packs, like the grazing yaks on the nature channel.

"Oh my god!" squealed Malia. "It's Connor Kelly."

Ever since fifth grade, Malia had been obsessed with Connor Kelly, which Bree could never quite figure out. Like, sure, he was kind of cute, but otherwise he reminded Bree of a turtle. He moved slowly around Playa del Mar, glancing around from time to time and not contributing much. Bree liked turtles the way she loved all animals, but it seemed like it might be hard to fall in love with one. But Connor had floppy hair and trendy sneakers, and when you're a thirteen-year-old boy, sometimes that was all you needed.

"I—I don't want him to see me like this!" Malia started obsessively touching her face, like it was covered with a swarm of honeybees.

"Don't want him to see you like what?" Bree asked.

"I'm not wearing any makeup! My hair is a mess! These pants are from last year!"

"You look exactly the same as you always do," said Dot.

Malia appeared to take major offense to this.

Still, in a show of solidarity, they all crouched behind the make-your-own-photo-strip booth, trying to hatch their next plan.

"Let's go to the toy store!" Bree said, pointing to the shop just in front of them. "You know, just to hide out. Until the boys pass by." This was a lie. Bree actually *wanted* to go to the toy store, because she secretly still liked it. But it had recently become unacceptable to shop there, and so Bree mostly kept this fact to herself.

"Good idea!" said Malia.

They scurried into the shop and immediately ducked into an aisle, safely out of sight.

"Wow," Bree said. "It's been so long since I was in here. I barely remember where anything is." None of this was true.

"Look! Bree, it's you!" said Dot. "The most enthusiastic creature in the animal kingdom!" She held up a stuffed golden retriever with glittery eyes. It was super cute and fluffy, with a pink tongue sticking sideways out of its mouth. Bree took it from her and gave it a little squeeze.

"Oh my god, Dot, that is like the nicest thing anyone's ever said to me!"

It seriously was. Golden retrievers were so sweet and nice and loyal. Not to mention popular. Bree bet that was the most popular breed there was. If she had to turn into an animal and couldn't be a housecat and also couldn't be a jungle cat, then she would definitely want to be a golden retriever.

"Should I buy it?" Bree asked. "Not to play with, um, but just to, like, commemorate this moment?" They both looked at her like she'd suggested getting a golden retriever tattooed on her face. "Okay, maybe I won't." Bree put it back down. "Bye-bye, doggy," she whispered.

"I bet the boys are gone by now. It's probably safe to move

on," said Dot, leading Bree and Malia back toward the front of the store.

But sure enough, Connor and his pack of surfers were standing right outside the entrance. They saw the girls surrounded by stuffed animals, and gave them the side-eye before roaming onward in the general direction of the food court.

Malia buried her face in her hands. "Oh my god. Connor Kelly thinks I'm a baby."

"Honestly, I wouldn't freak out about it. We're not even totally sure that Connor Kelly knows what your name is," said Dot.

Malia looked like she might hyperventilate.

"I know what will make you feel better. Let's go to Phoebe's!" Bree said.

Phoebe's was the most stylish, expensive store in the entire mall. It was where Bree's stepsister, Ariana, bought all her clothes, and where Bree dreamt of shopping as soon as she was old enough, or popular enough, or had enough money. She hoped today might be that day.

"I don't know, is Phoebe's really a good idea? We don't want to spend all our money before we've even started planning the party," said Malia.

"But we've already booked two more jobs!" Bree reminded her. "So there's plenty more where that came from."

"And we'll book a ton more soon," added Dot.

As soon as they entered Phoebe's, Bree saw it—the item that would finally make her cool.

It was a pair of sunglasses. But not just any sunglasses. Sparkly cat sunglasses. The oversize black frames formed little pointy cat ears in the top outside corners. The "ears" were encrusted with tiny black rhinestones. They were classy. They were glamorous. They were the most perfect use of plastic she had ever seen.

Bree slipped them on and craned to see herself in the display mirror.

"Please don't try on the merchandise unless you plan to buy it," came a voice of pure evil. Bree turned to see Camilla, a high school student she sort of recognized. She was a friend of Malia's big sister, Chelsea, and they sometimes rode to school together. Bree really didn't like her. Which is saying a lot, because she liked basically everybody.

"I'm planning to buy the sunglasses, thank you."

"How do you have enough money for those? You're, like, twelve."

63

"I *am* twelve, actually. Thanks for noticing. But if you must know, my friends and I have been babysitting and it's going quite well." She looked to her friends for backup, but they were each occupied in other sections of the store. Malia was in the process of trying on at least five different pairs of high-heeled shoes, while Dot was apparently grabbing every single item on display in the cosmetics section.

Camilla squinted her mean green eyes at Bree. "Really? How much money can you possibly make from babysitting?"

"A lot. It depends on the family. We have a job lined up later this week that's going to pay us, like, a ton."

Bree crossed her arms, satisfied with herself.

"That's so cute. Babies watching babies. I'm glad you guys have found yourselves a little hobby." She sashayed away and disappeared behind the register.

"Bree! Those glasses are so you," said Malia, clip-clopping over in a pair of giant platform sandals.

"Oh my gosh, yes," Dot agreed. She was struggling to hold six different tubes of expensive, perfumed deodorant.

"You guys, I think I'm living my best life!" Bree exclaimed.

By the time they left the mall, they had each found one small treasure. Dot also managed to consume a pizza slice, a cinnamon-sugar pretzel, and an enormous sundae with every single topping. "Because I have to load up while I can," she explained.

On their walk home, though, the guilt started to creep in.

"Should we have not bought anything?" asked Malia. "Like, I know we plan on making more money and all, but shouldn't we be saving it for the party?"

"Sounds like you have buyer's remorse," said Dot.

"I don't want to have remorse," Malia huffed. "I just want to have a party. But also look good while I plan it. Is that too much to ask?"

"It's too bad our special party can't be called a bat mitzvah," Bree said. She knew Charlotte said she had to study for, like, a really long time before hers, but still. It sounded so much cooler than a regular thirteenth birthday party.

"Yes, because none of us is Jewish," said Dot.

"Technically, I'm half Jewish," said Bree. "But I only celebrate Hanukkah every other year, when I spend the holidays with my dad."

Dot paused for a second, a thought playing across her face. "Maybe we can call it our *not mitzvah*."

"YES!" Malia shouted. "This can be our not mitzvah. As the director of marketing, this is definitely your finest work."

"You guys, we can't actually call it a not mitzvah," Dot said, crossing her arms. "I was making a joke."

"Well we won't put that on the invite or anything." Malia rolled her eyes. "But I think it has a nice ring to it."

"How much do you think it costs to have Taylor Swift perform at a not mitzvah?" Bree asked.

"Too much," said Dot.

"Think big!" chided Malia, then quickly added, "But yeah, way too much."

CHAPTER EIGHT

ALIA (NOT MALIA)

Lunch. Technically, it was just a thirty-minute stretch immediately following algebra. But to Malia, lunch was quite possibly the only redeeming part of the school day, and the only area in which she could ever be considered an over-achiever. She did her best to savor her successes, especially since they felt so few and far between. Every day, she'd sprint directly from class to the cafeteria and grab whatever meal was the day's special. Then she'd settle at her usual table in the front right corner and wait for the show to begin.

Connor Kelly usually arrived early to lunch, too. The high point of Malia's existence was watching him saunter up to the soft-drink vending machine. She'd watch as he inserted a dol-lar and pushed the buttons for B-7, the code that would shake loose a single can of iced tea–lemonade. She knew it sounded weird, but he did it so gracefully. His tan, surfery hands were weirdly manly for a seventh-grader. He'd pause for a moment, right there in front of the machine, crack open the can, and take a big sip. She'd never seen anything look so good. Ever.

Then Connor would disappear from sight, off to the back corner table, where only the cutest boys sat. Malia would dig into her lunch, pretending to be engrossed in her phone, until the rest of the gang showed up. Along with Bree, the usual lunch table consisted of four other girls: Stephanie, Ivy, Shoko, and Mo.

Bree was the first to arrive. As soon as she spotted Malia, she bounded over to the table.

"Alia! I haven't seen you in, like, three hours. I missed you."

"I have to say, I really appreciate your willingness to support my rebrand," Malia told her. She really meant it. Bree was probably the only person in Malia's life who made an effort to call her Alia.

"Of course!" Bree placed her tray on the table and sidled up for a hug.

"So, I have some news," Malia told her, just as Shoko and Mo shuffled up to the table. "I've had two more calls come in from the elementary school listserve."

"Oh my gosh, that's so great!" said Bree.

"Why are you guys working when you can just, like, ask your parents for money?" asked Mo. Mo wasn't trying to be mean. She just didn't know better. Her mom drove a Mercedes. Mo wore a new pair of shoes practically every single day. It was overwhelmingly clear that she couldn't feel their pain.

"Because working builds character," Malia lied. Her mom had told her this once.

Malia half-heartedly stabbed at her mac and cheese, a congealed glob more orange than any cheese she'd ever seen, in a shape that loosely resembled a brain. But then she remembered: thanks to babysitting, she would be able to buy new shoes, too. Things were only going to get better. Their next (and biggest) job with the Larssons was happening that very evening.

"We should tell Dot the latest!" said Bree.

At lunchtime, Dot always sat with her "school friends," the super-intellectual kids who wore mostly black and only took honors classes. They were a little weird, but mostly respected. In an odd way, they were even more powerful than the popular kids, because they retained an air of mystery, and people were a little afraid of them. Plus, they always knew the answers when they got called on.

Malia and Bree waited until Dot glanced in their general direction, then aggressively waved her over.

Malia saw Dot's shoulders move up and down in a sigh. It wasn't that Dot was embarrassed to be seen with them, exactly, but they usually kept their distance at school, especially at lunchtime, where interactions were highly specific and very isolated. Seventh-grade politics were complicated.

Dot's hair was in a messy braid and her artfully ripped black T-shirt read *Pink Floyd* on it. Another one of her elusive references. Who was this Floyd, and why was he pink?

"What's up?" Dot asked.

"We just wanted to let you know that we have two new jobs confirmed," Malia said. "So we are *set*."

As Malia spoke, Bree rummaged around in her backpack and pulled out a large folded-up piece of paper. She unfolded it again and again, until she'd unfurled an enormous chart, huge enough to contain a map of the world. Instead, it had at least two dozen photos of Taylor Swift glued all over it, along with glittery dollar sign stickers. In the center, there was a huge thermometer made out of colored paper, the kind you'd see at a fundraiser, showing how much money had been raised. *NOT MITZVAH!* was scrawled across the page in rainbow glitter glue. Apparently, Bree had taken it upon herself to construct the poster tracking the club's earnings.

"Dude, what's with all the Taylors?" Malia asked.

"I decorated it," Bree said with a shrug.

Dot's eyes shifted back and forth, her face glowing pink with embarrassment.

"Okay, so! This shows how well we're doing, financially speaking," Bree continued. "Right now we have zero dollars, since we already spent the money from the Woos, but after all the new jobs we've booked, we'll be back in business in no time. Of course, we have a ways to go until we can throw our party, but—"

"Bree!" Dot glanced around nervously. "Could we maybe do this later?"

"Oh! Yeah, sure." Bree started to fold up the Taylor map, but it was too late. Everyone else at the table was already engrossed in what they were saying, and a bunch of their classmates all over the cafeteria were now craning their necks to see what was going on.

"That does seem effective, what you guys are doing," said Dot a little too loudly.

"Are you trying to distance yourself from us?" Malia whispered.

Dot leaned in closer. "You guys know I love you, but this

71

is *lunch*. And I hate Taylor Swift. I don't want people to get the wrong impression," she hissed under her breath before giving them a wink and swiftly scurrying away.

Bree turned to Malia without missing a beat. "Alia, I just want you to know I'm so glad we're doing this together," she said. "I'm so proud of us. We're going to kill at the Larssons' tonight!" She paused for a moment before adding, "Not literally, of course."

Of course Malia had seen the Larssons' house before. Situated on a bluff overlooking the ocean, it was one of the biggest, most beautiful homes in the neighborhood, and nearly impossible to miss. In fact, it was *the* largest house in the whole town, second only to the Abernathy estate, which was owned by a crazy rich lady and was so big it looked like the White House. But Malia had never actually been close enough to touch it. Up close, it was *insane*. The massive gray building rose out of the ground and practically soared into the sky, like a castle. It was definitely worth hanging out with three small children if it meant a few hours of pretending to live here.

Bree, Dot, and Malia stood in front of the huge wooden front doors. Malia reached for the doorbell — a fancy metal situation that was shaped like King Triton — and waited. After a moment, the giant door swung open. But the face that greeted them wasn't Mrs. Larsson's.

"Chelsea! What are you doing here?"

Malia checked the number above the front door to make sure they had, in fact, gone to the right house. Yes, this was still 4 Sand Crab Way, home of the Larsson triplets.

Today was the correct date. They had arrived right on time.

So it made absolutely no sense why Malia's evil big sister had answered the door.

"The question is more like, what are *you* doing here?" Chelsea sneered down at Malia. "Shouldn't you be at home, being a child?"

"I am so confused. Why are you at the Larssons' right now?"

"Because I'm babysitting," she said.

"But . . . *we're* supposed to be babysitting."

Malia looked to her friends for backup. Dot and Bree put their hands on their hips and nodded their heads in agreement.

"Right." Chelsea tented her fingers. "About that. Camilla told me she saw you guys at the mall last week. And I thought, why should you be earning that kind of money when you're utterly unqualified?"

"Because it was my idea."

"Correction. It was *Kristy's Great Idea*. I saw that book in your room. You stole it from Kristy, and I stole it from you. Then I stole your phone. I intercepted a call from Dina Larsson confirming today's gig, and explained that I would be taking over. I also spoke with Mrs. Woo, to explain that we would be sitting for her girls in your place next Sunday. And now I'm going to put you out of business."

This was so typically Chelsea. Malia should have seen it coming. It was ironic, really. She seemed so perfect on the outside, but at her core, she was practically an insect.

"You — you — you suck!" said Bree.

Chelsea just smiled. "I have to say, the Larssons seemed kind of relieved to be leaving an actual teenager in charge. And you were right, they pay bank."

"I'm telling Mom!" This was, like, the worst comeback ever, but it was the only thing Malia could think of.

"Good luck with that, Malia." Malia swore Chelsea over-enunciated the *M* just to spite her. "Mom will totally take my side. I can drive. I wield a certain worldly authority. You're, like, twelve. No wait, you're literally twelve. Why would anyone trust *you* with their children?"

"Because we're nice?" Malia made a mental note to get better at comebacks.

Chelsea laughed a sinister laugh.

"Game over, baby babysitters. Go back to enjoying a life of puberty and poverty."

And with that, she slammed the door in their faces.

Bree frowned. "Wow, your sister is such a—"

"Yep. Ever since we were babies," Malia groaned.

"That just made me so glad I'm an only child," added Dot.

"What are we going to do?" Malia whined.

If Malia was being perfectly honest, she was actually kind of relieved that Chelsea was dealing with the Larsson triplets. Malia still wasn't particularly fond of booger eaters.

But then there was the issue of money. They were counting on the Larsson job as their biggest yet. They'd already spent every penny they'd earned, and Malia was no closer to throwing the most kickass party ever witnessed by the members of the seventh grade, including but not limited to one Connor Kelly.

Worst of all, though, being outsmarted by Chelsea was absurd and humiliating. Malia could handle being thrown out of the morning carpool or perpetually locked out of her room. She could deal with the fact that Chelsea was taller than her, and prettier than her, and that Chelsea had actual boobs. Malia could even get over that time Chelsea hid all her presents on

Christmas morning and told her that Santa didn't love her, or the time Chelsea started a rumor that Malia pooped in her bed (not true). And not to forget the time Chelsea secretly programmed her number into Malia's phone as "Connor Kelly" and texted her declarations of love, then died laughing when she believed them. Malia had *almost* gotten over that.

But this? This was too much. Malia may have been the average sister. But even average people deserved a victory, sometimes.

"Let's take her down," Malia said.

Malia didn't know how to fix it, but they had to find a way. No matter what happened, she couldn't let Chelsea win.

CHAPTER NINE

Dot

Dot sometimes forgot just how vast Bree's house was. It was one of the newer homes in the neighborhood, which went up after builders bulldozed a small beach cottage and crammed a giant monstrosity onto a not-so-huge lot. It had a fountain in the front yard and swirly trees cut like corkscrews lining the driveway. Every floor of the big white house was adorned with columns and balconies and terraces. It looked like a cross between a house and a wedding cake. Whenever they drove past, Dot's mom wrinkled her nose and said the tone of the neighborhood had really changed.

Bree and her four siblings each had their own room, and there were many more rooms beyond that—including a gym, a screening room, even a small bowling alley in the basement.

No matter how many times Bree invited Dot and Malia over, Dot sometimes still got lost.

Bree's bedroom, nestled onto the third and highest floor, was nearly the same size as Dot's entire bungalow. It had a walk-in closet, a canopy bed, a pink velvet couch, a cozy purple chair, a giant desk, a mirrored vanity for makeup and hair products, and a bunch of silver leather poufs scattered around for lounging. The center of the room was anchored with a giant, fluffy white area rug, where Dot, Malia, and Bree were sprawled, surrounded by bowls of candy. New money and white sugar—Dot's mom would have had a conniption.

Immediately following the disaster outside the Larsson house, Dot insisted they huddle for a very necessary crisis management meeting. As the head of marketing, it seemed like the right thing to do. It had only been twenty minutes since the whole debacle, but Dot had already stress-eaten approximately forty-five M&M's. Meanwhile, Bree was holding her cat like a rag doll and anxiously petting its fur. The cat looked perturbed, to say the least.

"Oh my god!" Malia exclaimed, scrolling around on her phone. "Chelsea added a link to her Instagram profile. For something called Seaside Sitters."

She clicked on the link and a beautiful website loaded onto the screen. With gorgeous professional photos, perfectly formatted text, and complementary shades of beachy blues, it was, quite possibly, the most well-designed site Dot had ever seen.

"When did they have the time to put this together?" Dot asked.

Somehow, Chelsea, Camilla, and their equally awful friend Sidney had managed to form something called the Seaside Sitters, a highly professional-seeming babysitters organization. At the top of the site, a group photo showed the three of them posing in front of a house with an actual white picket fence, looking clean-cut and beaming. Beneath it, a series of glamorous shots featured each babysitter laughing and frolicking with small children. They looked like stills from *The Sound of Music* but with jeans instead of lederhosen and beaches instead of Alps. The photos looked glossy and professional, like the entire operation. Dot wanted to throw up and die.

"They accept PayPal *and* Venmo?" Dot read. "And they offer services in *five* languages?" She scrolled further down the screen. "Oh my god, they even have an app so you can schedule your appointments right on your phone."

The more they scrolled, the worse it got.

"They undercut us! They're accepting lower rates! No wonder they're stealing our business."

"Dude, look at these testimonials!" said Malia.

"How can they have satisfied clients when they've been in business for two days?" asked Bree.

Need more reassurance?

We understand!

Your children are the most precious beings

on this planet, and we share your concerns.

Check out these real testimonials,

from just a few of our satisfied clients:

"These charming, talented, and responsible ladies go above and beyond!
My house looked cleaner when I returned than when I left.
They even organized the garage, just for fun!"
— Laura Glass

"Every time we hire Seaside Sitters, I am forced to ask myself:
are they babysitters, or wizards? Worth every affordable penny!"
— Henry McCormick

"Not only did the Seaside Sitters help our son Thor play Beethoven,
they're teaching all our boys to speak Dutch! Highly recommended!
Or, as my kids would say, *sterk aanbevolen!*"
— Erika Larsson

"Dude, what the—?" said Malia. "I am, like, totally flabbergasted."

"I know," Dot said. "Dutch is so not marketable."

"Um, the *Dutch* is what you're choosing to focus on here?" Malia snapped, turning on Dot like a rabid squirrel. "We don't even have a website! YOU were supposed to make one, 'Director of Marketing'!" She made air quotes with her fingers.

"Oh, please. Like our biggest issue here is our lack of a website. You're the one whose sister is actually the devil."

"The site might be just one of, like, seventy problems we have right now, but it's still *your* fault!"

Malia pointed her finger at Dot, who resisted the urge to bite it.

"You guys! Why are you freaking out?" said Bree, with an impossible amount of glee.

"Gee, I don't know, Bree. Why do you think we're freaking out?" Malia said, rolling her eyes. "We just lost what was only our second job, an evil organization is looking to take us down, we're still completely broke"—she turned to Dot before adding—"and we completely lack marketing materials."

"But I already made a website!" Bree said. Her tone was

how Dot imagined a friendly dolphin might sound, if a friendly dolphin could talk.

"Wait, you know how to code?" Dot asked.

"I mean, I looked some stuff up on the interwebs," she said. "Because I wanted to make us a landing page."

Dot had to admit, she was seriously impressed.

Bree pulled out her laptop, which was covered in glittery kitten stickers, and started typing away. A few seconds later, she turned the screen so it faced Dot and Malia.

"Ta-da!"

"Oh" was all Dot could manage to say.

Unbeknownst to them, Bree had gone and constructed the jankiest website in the history of the Internet. Whatever they were looking at appeared to have been created in Microsoft Paint. By a sloth. With a jumbo pack of markers and a head full of crazy dreams.

Photos of their three faces were awkwardly cut out and pasted onto stick bodies. Above their heads, a haphazard rainbow arched from one corner of the screen to the other. As if that wasn't weird enough, an image of Taylor Swift popped out from behind the rainbow, like a demented leprechaun overlord.

Just when Dot thought it couldn't get any worse, Bree scrolled down to show them the text portion of the site.

It didn't provide a phone number, email address, or any information that could possibly be useful to anyone. But it did end with a GIF of Taylor Swift, dressed in a skimpy leather outfit, winking and holding a phone.

Malia stared at it with her mouth hanging open.

"Um, as the director of marketing, you really should have run that by me," Dot said before taking deep, throaty breaths like Darth Vader. Without realizing it, Dot had started using the Ujjayi yoga breathing technique her mom had taught her to combat stress.

"Bree Alia Dot Babysitters," read Malia. "Is that, like, the best name we can come up with?"

"Whatever. Names don't have to make sense. Like, this

computer is called an Apple. But it's not a fruit, it's a computer," said Bree.

Dot blinked three times. "Yeah, but this may be the worst acronym ever."

"What do acrobats have to do with anything?" asked Bree.

"Not acro-bats. An acro-*nym*. When the first letter of each word spells out another name. Like FOMO."

Bree glanced back and forth between Malia and Dot, searching for some additional guidance. She twirled her hair around her finger, her sparkly nail polish glinting in the light.

"Bree!" Dot was exasperated at this point. "Look. At. The. Screen. Look at how the first letters of each of our names are enormous. Do you see what they spell?"

"B-A-D," spelled Bree.

Her eyes grew wide. Her mouth formed a perfect circle. She looked back and forth between Malia and Dot, as if one of them could possibly refute what her own hands had created.

Dot buried her head in her hands. "This literally says BAD. BAD Babysitters."

"But thanks for calling me Alia!" said Malia.

At least someone was happy.

CHAPTER TEN

MALIA*
(*THE "M" IS SILENT!!)

For as long as Malia could remember, every Thursday night was pizza night at the Twiggs residence. This was both good and bad. The good part was obviously pizza. The bad part was, well, everything else.

It's not that Malia disliked her family, exactly, but the whole group interaction usually left her feeling like the invisible sibling, even more than usual. This week, though, she had promised to set the record straight. This was the week she was going to tell her parents about the babysitters club, and about how Chelsea had stolen the idea right out from under her. This week Malia wanted someone to be proud of *her* for a change.

They usually ordered two large pizzas — one with all kinds of toppings, for Malia and her dad to share, and one boringly plain pie, for Chelsea and her mom. As soon as they settled into their seats and helped themselves to their first slices, Malia's mom asked the same question she did each week.

"So! Why don't you girls tell me about your days?"

"Dot and Bree and I—" Malia had barely gotten the words out when Chelsea started talking over her. Without fail, that also happened every single week. Sometimes Malia left the dinner table thinking she shouldn't bother to speak at all. In fact, she could probably replace herself with a cardboard cutout of herself, and none of her family members would notice. They would just think there was a lot of leftover pizza.

"Camilla and Sidney and I recently launched a premier childcare organization," Chelsea explained as she mopped the excess grease off her slice with a paper napkin.

"A childcare organization! Tell us more!" Their dad was beaming.

"Childcare is such an important topic, in our nation and the world at large," said their mom, nodding.

"That's why we've started a business to help local families with all their childcare needs. It's called the Seaside Sitters." Chelsea put her slice down on her plate, freeing up both hands to flip her long dark hair.

You know how in every animated movie ever, there's always that one character who's a villain, and you can tell because they have one mean characteristic, like squinty eyes or really dark eyebrows or a gold tooth that glints every time they say an evil thing? Malia often thought if her life were a movie, everyone would know Chelsea was evil by the way she constantly flipped her hair. She always did it whenever she said something particularly annoying.

"The Seaside Sitters! What a name!" said their dad, raising his lemonade glass in a toast. "I love the alliteration!" he added. Their dad was a high school English teacher, so this wasn't surprising.

"Thank you!" Chelsea replied, her tone all business. "The name was all me. But the branding and marketing is really more Camilla's territory. I'm the CEO, since I really want to be in control of the big picture."

"It's important to aim high," their mom said as she blotted the grease from her pizza. She was a career counselor at a nearby college, and she often said things like "aim high."

"I will never tire of being impressed by your entrepreneurial spirit," their dad chimed in.

"Gosh. It must feel so good to be in charge of your own creative endeavor!" added their mom. "Organized activities are great, of course, but there's something so empowering about launching your own brainchild."

"Actually, Chelsea got the idea from—"

"Malia, don't talk with your mouth full," their mom scolded.

Ugh. It wasn't even that full. Still, Malia swallowed her bite of pizza before continuing.

"What I was saying is that Chelsea actually stole the idea from—"

"Malia, all great ideas are somewhat derivative," Chelsea supplied before Malia could finish her sentence. "I mean, look at any amazing piece of art. Look at every single story ever told. Look at all the movies that are modern interpretations of classics. They've remade *Beauty and the Beast* like five times now. Nothing is entirely original. What is your point?"

Malia snorted. The point, of course, wasn't whether the idea was original. Malia had totally gotten it from a book, after all. The point was that Chelsea had stolen the idea *from her*, and then stolen *her* customers! And also, that Chelsea was perfectly okay sitting here and being celebrated for her supposed "genius," while Malia was made to feel more and more average by the second. The point was that Malia never ever got credit for anything.

"But just look at how you've taken this idea and run with it!" their dad piped up. "That's certainly original."

Malia sighed and took another bite of her pizza. What was the point? Even if she did tell them the entire story, her parents would never believe her. And even if they did, they would just find some way to side with Chelsea — that her execution of the idea was better, or that her website was more tasteful, or any number of countless things that made her better than Malia.

"One of our clients — you know Dina and Erika Larsson, who live in the giant house on the bluff?" Chelsea prattled on. "Anyway, Erika Larsson said part of the reason I'm such a fantastic sitter is because I also double as a tutor! I actually taught one of her sons how to do all of the math equations for the next three weeks' worth of upcoming chapters, so now he's ahead of the rest of his class! I'm really doing my part to shape young minds and ensure the success of the next generation."

Malia wasn't going to lie, that one almost made her hurl.

"Don't you think your sister is so inspirational?" gushed her mom.

"Yes," Malia said, smiling sweetly in Chelsea's direction. She smiled back at Malia, and reached up, once again, to tousle her own hair.

Malia chewed her pizza and started plotting her next move. So what if she had given up on this dinner conversation? She hadn't given up on destroying Seaside.

After dinner, she waited in her room with the door slightly ajar. When she heard Chelsea start running the shower, Malia tiptoed down the hallway, past their shared bathroom and into Chelsea's bedroom.

Chelsea's room was as perfect as she was—all the decor worked into her tasteful color scheme of navy blue and cream. Her books were neatly lined up on a shelf, alongside her impressive array of athletic trophies and academic awards. The bed was always made, which Malia found confusing. In fact, she had never seen it otherwise. It was almost like Chelsea didn't sleep.

Malia made her way to the desk and started rifling through drawers. Then she spotted Chelsea's backpack, hanging oh-so-neatly on a hook behind the door. So what if Chelsea had intercepted her phone? Two could play this game. And Malia was just getting started.

CHAPTER ELEVEN

Bree

Ever since Bree accidentally called them the BAD Baby-sitters, everything in the universe had been that way —very, very bad. Obviously the whole thing was just a mistake, but Malia and Dot spent the entire next day acting kind of mad at Bree, which made her sad, as her best friends were all of the non-cat things she loved about this world.

So when Malia texted saying to meet her at Marvelous Ray's, Bree was so, so, so excited. Not just because she was maybe forgiven, but also because Marvelous Ray's was easily the best place on earth. They had arcade games and Skee-Ball and music and dancing and candy and pizza and joy. Plus, boys always hung out there, if you were into that kind of thing.

When Bree got there, she had the same feeling she always had when entering Marvelous Ray's, which was kind of like when you first see a Christmas tree with all the presents underneath it and are like, "OH-MY-GOD-SO-MUCH-HAPPINESS-WHERE-DO-I-BEGIN?" Bree was hungry and wanted fries. She also wanted to play the mermaid ring toss game, because the prizes for that one were all super glittery and they changed them all the time. But when she opened the door, Malia was standing right inside the entrance, next to the giant statue of a manatee wearing a T-shirt, which was the Marvelous Ray's mascot. Her arms were crossed and she had the same expression she had whenever she got into a fight with Chelsea, where her lips formed a straight line across her face.

"Dot is already here. Go order food and then meet us in the back corner," Malia commanded. It was honestly pretty scary. "We have business to discuss."

Bree let out a sigh. So the mermaid ring toss game would have to wait. She ordered fries and, while they were cooking, went to take a very quick peek at the new prizes. Two words: "GLITTER CONVERSE." Okay, one more word: "PURPLE."

Then she picked up her plastic basket of fries and made her way to the back corner to find her friends. Malia and Dot were already sitting at one of the little neon orange tables. Dot's tray was loaded with enough food to feed all of Bree's siblings at once and then maybe also the entire boys' soccer team. There were French fries, sweet potato fries, chicken fingers, a cheeseburger, and an order of fried Oreos. Dot caught Bree eyeing her food with wonder.

"What? I had a gift card for winning the grand prize at science summer camp, so I kind of ordered everything."

"You and your science fairs," said Malia.

"You are welcome to partake. Whatever I don't finish is coming home in my purse." Dot turned her attention back to Malia, who nervously drummed her fingers on the table. "Okay. What's up?"

"I have done reconnaissance!" Malia announced, jumping out of her chair.

"Like Leonardo da Vinci?" Bree asked. Ariana was in the high school's art history class and was always talking about the Reconnaissance.

"Bwee," said Dot, through a mouthful of chicken finger. It was like she was so excited about both fried poultry and the chance to share her knowledge that she couldn't decide what came first. "Leonardo da Vinci is from the *Renaissance*. Malia is talking about *reconnaissance*. Which means, like, spying."

"Oh," Bree said. She had thought she was right, but whatever. She wouldn't have to take art history for, like, five more years.

"As ALIA was saying," Malia continued, pacing back and forth in front of the pick-a-prize crane game that no one ever actually won. "I have done reconnaissance and the news is not good. I looked through Chelsea's desk while she wasn't home. And maybe also the contents of her backpack. And maybe also her phone while she was showering. The Seaside Sitters have taken all of the business in town. They have jobs booked for days, weeks, *months*, even. They're working for every family I've ever heard of, plus some from the next town over. There is nothing left for us. We are basically out of business."

All three of them sighed.

"Well, that's sad," Bree said.

"Why are you deciding to break this news at the temple of joy?" Dot asked, sweeping her arm overhead, where a million happy lights blinked back at them.

"Because that's where it gets interesting. My friends, this place is our future," said Malia, triumphantly putting her pointer finger up in the air.

Bree looked at Dot. She seemed as confused as Bree was. Was Malia suggesting they ditch babysitting and get jobs at

Marvelous Ray's? Because she would totally be into that, if working at age twelve wasn't illegal.

"You guys," Malia continued. "Do you remember that day in the gazebo? When I found the book and those weird little kids were doing the thing with the boogers?" Dot and Bree nodded.

"Do you remember what that felt like?"

"The booger part? That was gross," Bree said.

"Not the booger part. The part where the three of us joined together to create something new. We decided to form this club because we wanted money for a party and because employment is empowering and also because it seemed like it would be sort of nice to do something with each other where we could hang out and get paid for it. But more importantly, we made this club because it was something bigger than all of that. *It was our dream.*"

Malia had this crazy look in her eyes that reminded Bree of the time she drank an entire can of lemonade in one gulp right after gym class, and then got sick a few minutes later.

"I mean, the word 'dweam' might be a little stwong," said Dot, her mouth completely full of cheeseburger. Malia glared at her. Dot swallowed. "Or, yeah, I guess you could call it a dream."

"And what do we know about dreams?" Malia asked.

"Sometimes they're scary?" Bree said. She always had the same dream over and over again, where her family was on a road trip and they forgot her at an ice cream stand in the middle of the desert and she had to learn to live all by herself, just her and the cacti.

"Guys." Malia threw her hands up in the air. "I'm not talking about nightmares! I'm talking about dreams! I'm talking about the kind of dreams where just thinking about them makes you want to cry, but in a good way! Like, Bree, when you guessed all the jelly beans in the jar. Or, Dot, all the food that is slowly but surely making its way into your mouth right now. Or the way I'll feel when Connor Kelly finally tells me he loves me!"

Malia clamped one hand over her mouth and looked around in panic. She had totally been yelling, and anyone could have just heard her admit her crush. Luckily, everyone was absorbed in some activity and didn't seem to care. She continued her speech but slightly quieter this time.

"Dreams are everything in life! Without them, we're just blobs with feet that go to school and do a bunch of stuff we don't really want to do. We can't vote. We can't even drive! But we can look after children who are smaller than us. And we can throw a party. At Marvelous Ray's."

"We can?" Bree asked. She didn't know they could do that.

"Yes. That is why we're here. I added us to the waitlist for the Marvelous Pizza Party Package. Usually they're all booked up for at least a year, but something magical has happened. Somebody canceled. And we can have our very own marvelous soiree. In just three weeks, right after the fall break."

Bree's heart started to beat really fast, the way it did before a math test.

"How are we supposed to pay for it without babysitting?" asked Dot. "As previously discussed, my mom can't afford to help out."

"And my parents said they'll chip in the usual amount, but they can't pay for the entire thing," Bree added.

"We can still raise the money IF we find a way to win back the business that should be ours," said Malia. Dot did not look convinced. "You guys. This isn't just about money!" Malia continued. "This is about DREAMS! Like throwing a party that will make everyone in the seventh grade super impressed! Like actually doing a thing better than your sister! Like finally having people take you seriously! Like the three of us celebrating our birthdays right here, with pizza!"

Slowly, Dot and Bree started nodding.

"With that weird giant manatee statue as my witness, we

will take down the Seaside Sitters!" Malia pledged. "We will babysit all the children! And we will throw the best party that Playa del Mar has ever seen!" She grabbed a fry and held it overhead. "Who's with me?"

Dot and Bree each grabbed a fry and joined them with Malia's, like the fast-food equivalent of knights clanking swords.

"To dreams!" said Malia, holding her fry aloft for another moment before victoriously cramming it into her mouth.

"You're insane," said Dot. But she smiled as she, too, ate her fry.

"I . . ." Bree started.

"Yes?" Malia ventured, midchew.

"You . . ." Bree tried again.

"What's up?" asked Dot.

"To dreams!" Bree said, before making a sound kind of like a hiccup. She didn't say anything else, but she didn't have to. Bree was crying, in a good way.

CHAPTER TWELVE

MALIA

I t was time to develop a plan of attack.

The three of them were gathered in Dot's living room, which smelled the way it always did: like some sort of burning sage bush landed inside a health food store. Dot's mom had created a spread of snacks, which were scattered in little brass bowls all over the low wooden coffee table. There were weird green balls rolled in sesame seeds, some kind of nut Malia had never seen before, and shriveled dried dates that resembled bugs. Last but not least, one of the bowls contained—no joke—twigs. Malia didn't know what they tasted like, and she wasn't about to find out.

"So how are we supposed to generate business?" Dot asked, suspiciously eyeing a twig.

"Part of the problem is that Seaside isn't just older and

taller and equipped with vehicles — their rates are way lower than ours," Malia grumbled. "So if we want to be competitive, we have to go even lower."

"Yeah, but, we don't want to have to work for nothing," Dot said. "As we've discovered, babysitting actually requires effort. We have to charge what our services are worth."

"But working for almost nothing is better than making nothing at all!" Bree chimed in.

"I'm not sure our ideologies are going to align on this one," Dot said.

"Hmm?" said Bree, wrinkling her forehead.

"Like, I think we have different ideas about how to run the business," Dot explained.

Bree reached for one of the twigs and popped it into her mouth. Malia watched her, chewing slowly and with effort. She had probably only taken a twig so Dot's mom wouldn't feel bad that the food went untouched. Bree was so nice.

"Maybe there's an in-between," Malia started. "Maybe we can charge a super-low rate, but just as a special trial. So we'll tell people to try us out for even less than what Seaside is charging. Then, if they like us, we raise our rates so they're right in line with Seaside."

"I guess that sounds all right," said Dot. "But we've already blasted the listserve and it doesn't seem to be working. How do we actually get customers?"

"I think we get out there and talk to people face-to-face. Go door-to-door. Hand out flyers. Stand outside the Playa del Mar-ket," Malia suggested.

"Ooh! Can I be the one who stands outside the market?" Bree visibly brightened.

"Does this have to do with that creepy mechanical horse ride you like so much?" Malia asked.

"You guys, I've totally outgrown that," said Bree. And then two seconds later added, "Okay, yeah."

"Bree, you cannot ride the horse when we're out looking for business," Malia said. "The point is to look mature and col-lected, like Seaside."

Bree sighed. "All right, no carousel horse. I promise."

Later that afternoon, flyers in hand, the three of them headed off to divide and conquer. Bree went to stand in front of the Playa del Mar-ket, while Malia took a lap around the neigh-borhood. Dot had to go to a meeting about the school's up-coming fall science fair, but she promised to take on any job they found for her.

First, Malia approached the house at the end of the

cul-de-sac. It was a tiny ranch with white siding and powder-blue shutters. The bushes lining the front walkway had been manicured into little leafy balls, like something out of *Alice in Wonderland*.

She knocked on the door. A man popped his head out of the door. He wore huge round glasses that made him look sort of like an owl.

"'Ello?" he practically yelled, even though Malia was less than two feet away.

"Good afternoon, sir! My name is Malia and I'm with an organization called Best Babysitters!" The rebrand was a spur-of-the-moment decision, but once the name was out of her mouth, she had to admit it had a nice, alliterative ring to it.

"Sitters? I like sitting!" the man shouted.

"Yes! Um, sitting is very necessary, I suppose." This was shaping up to be a weird interaction. Malia thought about running away but it seemed rude, so she just stood there, awkwardly digging her toe into the welcome mat.

"That's what I say! What's wrong with sitting? But people keep trying to sell me one of those standing desks."

"Huh?"

"What are you here for?" He squinted at Malia. "Are you trying to sell me something? I hope it's not a desk."

"No! Well, I mean, yes. I mean, my friends and I have a babysitting service and we're offering a special right now."

"I don't have any babies." The man seemed perturbed.

Malia inched away. "Sorry to disturb you! Thank you for your time!" she called as she scurried down the front pathway.

Okay, then, she thought. That was special.

Malia headed to the next house over. It was a small brick home, and she didn't really know who lived there, but there were always tricycles littering the front yard, so they had to have kids. A friendly woman opened the front door. Her hair was actually yellow. Not blond, yellow.

"Hi! My name is Alia and I wanted to let you know about my babysitting—" Before she could even finish her sentence, the woman cut her off.

"Are you with the Seaside Sitters? I just read something *lovely* about that organization on the class parents' message board."

Malia's heart sank, but she did her best to maintain a delightful, professional expression.

"Um, no, I'm actually part of a different organization, called Best Babysitters." The woman's face grew noticeably disinterested, but Malia kept right on talking. "We take our jobs very seriously. In fact, we've been operating even longer than the Seaside Sitters. We're the original babysitters. Anyway! We're having a special promotion right now that I'd love to tell you more about."

She went on to explain their super-discounted rates and their bottomless love for small children. At first the woman seemed into it, but after a moment, her face twisted into a look of disbelief. It was like she was almost suspicious of just how little Malia was charging.

"Do you guys also watch pets?" she asked.

"Uhh, that's not really our specialty, but I guess we could?" Malia said.

"We're headed out of town next week as a family, so the kids won't be here. But we'll need someone to come feed our cat, Stanley. You'd only have to stop by a couple times a day."

Cat feeding? It sounded weird to Malia, but Bree would be all over that.

"Sure! That sounds wonderful!" Malia said.

This was going to be easier than she thought. She had only knocked on two doors so far, and already had booked a client! Granted, it was for an entirely different species than the one they had set out to care for, but as Dot's mom liked to say, sometimes the best things in life are the ones you didn't plan for.

CHAPTER THIRTEEN

Dot

For most of Dot's life, her mother had been telling her to follow her "inner compass." When Dot was seven, her mom went so far as to buy Dot an actual compass and string it onto a necklace, as a reminder to follow her internal one. The thing about a compass is, it doesn't tell you if you're headed the right way. It just points in the general direction you're going, and wobbles around a lot, practically mocking your every move. But Dot guessed she appreciated the symbolism.

Anyway, the Best Babysitters Club—or whatever they were calling it this week—had become a prime example of what happens when one does not follow one's internal compass. Dot had always been crystal clear about her lukewarm feelings toward small children, ongoing responsibility, and group projects (which left little room for individual creativity to flourish). Yet she agreed to this club because she shared her friends' desire for an amazing party, and she liked the idea of hanging out with them for profit.

Still, Dot's love for her friends couldn't change the facts. They weren't really earning any money. They were no closer to having the budget to throw a joint birthday. When the party never materialized, they would be embarrassed in front of the entire seventh grade. The Seaside Sitters were making life stressful. And their friendship would continue whether they babysat or not.

Yet here Dot was, knocking on the door of one Mabel Mc-Mimmers, a new client who Bree discovered in front of the Playa del Mar-ket. The door opened to reveal a tiny old lady. She wore a bright purple top and matching purple pants, with green paisleys frolicking all over them. She looked like a grape at a disco. A long strand of green beads completed the ensemble. She peered at Dot.

"Hello there, young lady. Are you Dot?"

"I am. Are you Mrs. McMimmers?"

"Yes. Come in, come in! Please, call me Mabel."

She opened the door wide enough so Dot could enter. Dot

followed her (ever so slowly) down the corridor. The walls were covered in pink floral wallpaper. Big pink flowers blossomed as far as the eye could see.

Mabel was approximately one million years old. Okay, fine, that might be a slight exaggeration, but may it suffice to say that she fell safely in the great-grandparent category. Her hair formed a helmet of little white curls, which clung tightly to her head. It looked crunchy, sprayed straight through with hair spray, like you could hold a fan right up to her head and it wouldn't move at all. Was Dot here to watch her grandkids?

At the end of the hallway, Mabel turned right and they entered a bright window-lined living room. Green plants were everywhere—hanging from hooks, lining the floors, all over the shelves covering one of the walls. There were more leaves in this room than she'd ever seen in one place, but no toys to speak of. No tiny shoes. No childlike sounds. No colorful books. No sign of children at all.

"So, who will I be sitting today?" Dot asked. This seemed like a fair question.

"My darlings!" Mabel said, opening her arms wide.

Dot looked around once more, for good measure. She saw no darlings. Not even one. Her heart caught in her throat as she wondered if she had unwittingly stepped into a horror movie. Dot should have known better than to accept a referral from Bree, sight unseen. She started to picture the headlines in the *Playa del Mar Sunday Star*: *Local Girl Goes Missing, Held Hostage by Elusive "Darlings."*

"The plants need constant attention," Mabel clarified.

"The—plants?" Hold the phones, Dot was watching *plants?* What was there to watch? Plants don't even move.

"Yes, it can be hard for me to reach some of them these days. And to carry the watering can. Honestly, it's getting harder for me to do a lot of things that used to be simple." She smiled sweetly, and Dot couldn't help it, her heart smiled back. "That's why today's plant-sitting training is so very important," she concluded. And just like that, Dot's heart stopped smiling.

"Plant-sitting . . . training?" Dot asked.

Did Bree not ask this woman any questions?

"Yes! All the plants have very specific needs." Mabel pointed to the bookshelf and started calling out individual plants. "Vladimir can be very feisty, and Jonas only gets watered every other week, but likes to be misted very often. Caitlin needs lots of water and so does Penelope." She looked back at Dot. "Are you taking notes, dear? This is very important."

Dot riffled around in her backpack and pulled out her little red notebook, which was usually reserved for recording angsty thoughts and observations of the natural world. She supposed that on some level, this wasn't all that different from an environmental science class.

"Okay. Now. Fiona is the fiddle-leaf ficus, and her needs can be very fickle. Fickle fiddle Fiona! Fiona the ficklest fig!" Mabel clapped her hands.

Dot wrote: *Fiona. Impossible to please. Stay away.*

Mabel prattled on.

"The pencil cactus is named Leslie, because she reminds me a bit of my sister-in-law. All limbs, that one."

Dot wrote: *Leslie. Pencil cactus. Sister-in-law?*

"Rebecca is the rhododendron. She should really be outside, but I haven't gotten around to having her replanted. You can help with that!"

Dot wrote: *Bree can replant Rebecca.*

Next, Mabel rattled off an incredibly long list of names. These were her beloved succulents, which lined the windowsill. The good news was they didn't require much water or care. The bad news was, she insisted Dot address them by name. In alphabetical order.

When they were done with all of this, Mabel said it was time for Dot's quiz. "It's very important to determine that you've passed the training before I let you interact with my darlings," she explained, like all of this was normal.

"Who is the ficklest fig?"

"Um, Fiona?"

"Very good! Now let's run down the list of succulents, in the proper order."

"Abraham, Brian, Eloise, Frank, Helen, Jacques, Louis, Paul, Reynaldo, and Ziggy." Dot had read the names directly from her notes, but Mabel didn't seem to care.

"That's marvelous! Oh, that's just marvelous," she said. "I am so pleased. I can't wait until our next engagement. Maybe next time we can share some tea? I'd love to hear more about school and what you're up to."

"Sure," Dot said. She didn't know how to feel about this endeavor. It was super weird and not at all what she'd bargained for, but she got the sense that Mabel was in need of a friend. Maybe Dot could help out with her plants if it brought Mabel joy. Dot's mom would say this was an opportunity to create good karma.

"That other young lady agreed today's training was without charge," Mabel explained. Dot took a deep breath. Bree had said today's job was for free? "But as a thank-you for your time, here is a seedling for you to care for." Mabel pressed a tiny potted plant into Dot's hands. "You may name her whatever you wish."

Dot stared down at the little plant. It was green, but it sure wasn't cash.

CHAPTER FOURTEEN

MALIA

At least there was still something good about the world, Malia thought as she watched Connor Kelly sashay across the front of the cafeteria. His jeans reminded her of a cowboy and a motorcyclist and a rock star and a skater, all in one. How did he do it? How did he look good in everything, always?

He paused in the middle of the room, like the world was his stage, and brushed his floppy bangs back off his forehead. His hair had a magical ability to appear both full and soft at the same time. Malia wanted to know what it felt like.

She sighed as this most glorious of visions was suddenly interrupted by a less glorious one: Bree and Dot approaching, lunch trays in hand. So Dot was actually sitting with them, in full view of everyone, from the start of lunch? This was interesting.

"What's the matter?" asked Bree as soon as she saw Malia. "You look really sad."

"Yesterday's babysitting job was the worst thing I have ever experienced," Malia said. It wasn't an exaggeration. She had been tasked with watching an angry baby who screamed and screamed for no apparent reason. It had been a test of her sensibilities, and also her senses. Her head was still ringing from the din of yelling baby.

"Really? Because I'll bet I have you beat," challenged Dot.

"My friends, I have just two words." Malia paused for dramatic effect. "Baby diarrhea."

"EEEEEEEWWWWWWWWWWWWWW!" they both shrieked in unison.

"Oh, yes. Yesterday I learned that 'babysitting' takes on a whole new meaning when the child is actually a baby. When it is a baby that's recently eaten some kind of mushy pea puree that violently disagrees with its system, it's basically something out of a horror movie. To make matters worse, the kid kept screaming, and I tried absolutely everything I could to calm him down. But nothing worked! And then the parents didn't

113

even seem grateful! As soon as the mom picked him up, he quieted down, and she looked at me like I was defective. Please tell me your days were better," Malia said.

Dot plucked a tiny potted plant from her cafeteria tray and placed it in the center of the table. "This is Bartholomew. He is a mung bean sprout, which was my payment for plant-sitting training, which is what I spent yesterday doing." She glared at Bree. "Did you not ask Mabel what the job even entailed?"

Bree looked thoughtful for a moment. "Hmm. She said she had almost twenty darlings. I guess if she had meant children that would have been kind of a lot."

"How was your job, Bree?" Malia asked, to change the subject before Dot could kill her.

"Oh, it was wonderful!" said Bree. "Stanley is such a nice cat, and I gave him both wet food and dry food, and I cleaned his litter box. I have to stop by twice a day, and it's so fun. And when I went there the first time to meet him and pick up the keys, his owners said this could even become a regular thing!"

"That's great!" Malia said. "And you're cat-sitting this whole week, right? So how much does that add up to?"

"Well, that's the thing . . ." Bree trailed off.

"What's the thing?" Malia asked.

"I think Stanley's owners kind of misunderstood the special

offer. They seemed to think I would watch him this week free of charge, as, like, a trial. And I felt super weird correcting them, so I said that was fine. Because it's so fun! It doesn't even feel like work, really."

Malia put her head down on the table and sighed. This was a disaster. She had canvassed the entire neighborhood, and all they had come up with amounted to poop, plants, and volunteer work. Had this whole club idea been a mistake? Just a few weeks ago, it seemed like a party was the answer to everything. It would make them feel cool and popular and relevant. Plus, it would be fun. But if babysitting wouldn't yield the funds, they were left with no choice. Maybe deciding to have no party was better than torturing themselves.

Malia groaned. If the club disbanded, Dot would still have her honors friends and all sorts of science fairs to look forward to. Bree had her uplifting interest in musicals and her satisfying obsession with cats. But what did Malia have? The sort of secret truth was, screaming babies aside, she actually *liked* babysitting. Or more accurately, she liked being the CEO. Without the club, what was Malia left with?

Malia picked her head up, expecting to see her friends' worried faces, but instead, she saw a swath of denim. It looked like a cowboy and a motorcyclist and a skater and ALL OF HER

DREAMS and it was less than a foot from her face. Malia looked skyward, until she could see the face that was attached to the body. Somewhere, an angel sang.

"I heard you're having some kind of party," said Connor Kelly.

And just like that, the party was back on.

Malia wanted to say yes. Yes, Connor, of course there would be a party. She wanted to tell him everything they'd been planning, and how it would be at Marvelous Ray's, and how it would have all of the best activities, and food, and prizes, and how it would be the perfect venue for Malia and Connor to finally realize their romance was meant to be. But Connor Kelly. Was talking. To her. On purpose. So she sort of panicked, and the word that came out of her mouth was something similar to "Meep?"

"Well, I love parties. Keep me posted, Malia," he said, and sauntered away.

She stared after him as he exited the cafeteria. He really did look good from all angles.

"He called you Malia," said Dot. "Don't you want to correct him?"

"You know, I kind of like the name Malia," Malia said.

Hearing it come out of Connor's mouth, it sounded like a really nice name, after all.

"Earth to Alia," said Dot. Of course, now she finally decided to call her Alia.

"Connor Kelly is coming to our party," Malia said. They were the most beautiful words she had ever said out loud.

"Well, right now there is no party, unless Marvelous Ray's accepts payment in bean sprouts."

"We still have time!" Malia said. "All is not lost. We just need to get creative."

"Dude, I had to sing a song about a fiddle-leaf ficus," Dot said, crossing her arms. "How creative do you want us to get?"

"I love you for doing that," Malia said, flashing Dot her best smile.

"Malia—I mean, Alia—I mean, Malia—is right," said Bree. "We can definitely figure out a way to make this party happen!"

"That's the spirit!" Malia said. Because it was true. Everyone was already talking about the party, and there was so much on the line. They couldn't give up now. This was a chance to look cool, to feel popular, to show everyone—including

Connor Kelly and Malia's evil sister and everyone else who had ever overlooked Malia — that she was part of something amazing. Maybe even that she *was* amazing. "I bet the job of our dreams will turn up when we least expect it," Malia said, in a tone that she hoped would encourage the universe to make it so. "We just have to believe."

CHAPTER FIFTEEN

Bree

The only thing more fun than shopping for glittery things to wear during your everyday life is shopping for glittery things to wear on special occasions. This included glitter dresses, glitter purses, glitter shoes, glitter jewelry (obviously), and glitter tiaras. Bree's stepsister, Ariana, once told her that tiaras weren't really appropriate to wear to social occasions unless you're royalty like Kate Middleton, but Bree disagreed. That might be the only fashion advice where Bree thought Ariana was totally wrong.

Anyway. Bree had already touched all the above items at the Playa del Mar Mall, where Malia, Dot, and Bree were browsing for stuff to wear to their epic party. They still hadn't found any new money, and they still hadn't booked any new jobs, but Dot's mom was always telling them about the power of visualization, so they decided to try it out. Visualization is where you picture amazing things that haven't happened yet, and you feel how happy you'll be once they happen, and then, kind of like magic, they come true. If they made friends with all the things they couldn't buy yet, they reasoned, then soon enough maybe they could buy them. The more they visualized, the closer they would be to the bash of their dreams.

"It's a thirteenth birthday party, not a sweet sixteen," Malia said, eyeing the extra-large crown on top of Bree's head.

"Yes, and this party is whatever we want it to be, remember?" It was true. They had encouraged each other to think big. Still, Bree took the tiara off her head and placed it carefully back on the shelf, next to a bunch of other sparkly hair items. "I'm coming back for you," she whispered, low enough so no one else could hear.

"This is depressing!" Dot chimed, appearing from behind a rack of dresses. "I know we're supposed to be visualizing or whatever, but I still can't afford any of this, never mind the fees for a party. I think we might benefit from a break."

Part of the problem was that they were in Lovely Days, which was a bridal store, and a place where they did not belong. They couldn't go back to browsing at Phoebe's, for fear of running into evil Camilla, so they were forced to settle for the next best thing. Lovely Days sold bridal gowns, of course, and also fancy dresses people wore for things like proms and sweet sixteens and actual bat mitzvahs. Everything was sparkly! But everything was expensive.

"Let's go to the cat café!" Bree suggested. The cat café was a newer addition to the mall and had quickly become her favorite place. She loved it even more than the toy store, partially because she could be totally open about how much she loved it.

"Why do they call it a cat café?" Malia asked as they walked toward it. "They have cats but no food. And you definitely can't eat the cats."

"It's definitely not a café," Dot confirmed. "It's more like a cat party that humans can crash."

They opened the doors to MeowTown, and Bree's heart practically exploded with joy. There were orange cats and gray cats and white cats and black cats and black-and-white cats and even one hairless cat, which was kind of scary-looking but Bree still loved it, of course, because it was a cat.

"This entire room is like one big histamine," said Dot.

"What's a histamine?" Bree asked.

"It's an organic compound that produces a response in the body," Dot responded.

"STOP SPEAKING SCIENCE," commanded Malia.

Ever since Dot had been accepted into the honors science class at the start of the school year, she had a tendency to nerd out even more than usual about sciencey things. No one else ever understood what she was talking about.

"It's, like, the technical name for the thing that makes people feel allergic to stuff," Dot explained.

"HI, GERALDINE!" Bree yelled, scooping up a gray tabby. Bree had met Geraldine the last time she came to the cat café, with her little sisters and brother. Bree smushed her face into the cat's soft, soft fur.

"How do you already know their names?" asked Dot.

"She comes here a lot," said Malia, before Bree even had a chance to answer.

Dot sat down on one of the benches and distantly petted an orange cat, using just two fingers. "Hello, kitty," she said in a businesslike tone. The cat meowed back at her.

Malia clapped her hands. "So, guys, now that we've visualized, we should really talk about our plans moving forward. Bree can hopefully turn cat sitting into a regular side gig. And it sounds like Mabel wants somebody to hang out with, to water her plants or . . . whatever. But both of those things pay basically no dollars. And neither of these things are what we set out to do—babysitting."

"Certainly we must have more leads," Dot chimed in. "Let's list all the families we've sat for in the past. Who can we call and check in with?"

"Um . . . the Woo kids?" Bree asked.

"According to Chelsea's calendar, they've been using Seaside on the regular. But it couldn't hurt to ask," said Malia.

"Bree, what about the parents of your little siblings' friends? Do you think we can reach out to some of them?"

Before Bree had a chance to answer, a lovely voice interrupted them.

"Excuse me, did I hear you girls talking about babysitting?"

Bree looked up to see a woman standing before them, holding a white longhaired cat. That alone would have been enough to make Bree love her, but she also looked really pretty and soft and nice, kind of like an angel from a movie. The woman's hair was blond and curly and she was wearing a short-sleeved pink sweater that was sort of fluffy. Bree wanted to pet her, and then pet the cat she was holding, and then give both of them a big hug.

"Yes!" Bree exclaimed. "I'm Bree, and this is Dot and Malia—I mean, Alia. The three of us have a babysitting club."

"It's so nice to meet you. My name is Wendy Blatt, and my son and I recently moved to Playa del Mar."

"Wendy! That's such a nice name," Bree said. "It's actually my favorite name, because of *Peter Pan*." Dot shot her a look like that was a weird thing to say, but Wendy just smiled sweetly.

"Thank you," she said. "When I was growing up, I never met another Wendy, but now that I'm an adult I really like it. Anyway, my son, Aloysius, just turned five."

Bree had definitely never met anyone named Aloysius, like, ever, but she didn't say so.

"He's a very sensitive soul," Wendy continued. "Very bright for his age, and it's been tough on him to be the new kid. Adjustments can be so hard, and kids aren't always the nicest."

It reminded Bree of back when she had been the new kid. That definitely wasn't easy. It was right after her mom had married Marc, and she was just getting used to living in a new house, in a new town. On top of it all, once school started she'd spent the first few weeks feeling confused and friendless. Then one day, the chorus teacher, Ms. Hedinger, made everyone sing "Ging Gang Goolie" in front of all the first-graders at the harvest assembly. Bree grew flustered and forgot the words. She was about to cry, but Dot and Malia were standing on either side of her, and they sang extra loud to make up for it. Bree had been able to move her mouth, silently mouthing the word "watermelon" over and over again, and everything had been fine. That was the first time she knew her friends were wonderful.

"Anyway, Aloysius has been staying at the after-school program, and participating in some extracurriculars for gifted children, but I think it would be best if he could work on his hobbies in a quiet environment."

"That sounds like a perfect plan," said Dot, folding her hands in her lap and nodding confidently.

"Ideally, I'd love to find someone to watch him after school every day, just until I get home from work. Maybe you girls could spend some time with him, and if you all get along, we can figure something out?"

"Yes!" they all said in unison. What could be better than a smart kid with an interesting name and quiet hobbies? Well, Bree supposed cat-sitting would be better, but this was pretty great, too.

"In fact, you can meet him right now. There he is!" Wendy motioned to a far corner of the café, where a little boy sat alone, perfectly quiet. He wore all-black clothes, like a tiny poet, and he was surrounded with cats. Like, two cats were perched on his lap, and another was wrapped around his shoulders like a furry scarf. Bree seriously admired his skills. Was he some kind of cat whisperer?

"Hey there, Aloysius," said Malia.

"Hello," he said, so quietly they could barely hear him. His eyelashes were so long that when he blinked, it looked like butterflies were fluttering down his face. He seemed like a sweet kid, and quite possibly, the ideal client. They made plans for a trial babysitting job the very next day.

"Wow," Bree breathed as soon as they'd left the cat café. "Visualization really works."

"I think that was more like happenstance." Dot shrugged.

Whatever it was, how lucky were they? Just when they thought they might be out of business, their dream client had walked right into their lives. Holding a cat! Bree couldn't help but feel like this was meant to be.

CHAPTER SIXTEEN

MALIA

Where is Dot?" Malia asked aloud, texting her for what felt like the millionth time.

"She said her meeting might run late." Bree shrugged.

The fall science fair was fast approaching, which meant Dot had been spending more and more time with her weird, beaker-wielding honors friends, and less time with Malia and Bree.

But today was their first time babysitting Aloysius, and they needed to do everything in their power to ensure the gig went well. For this initial job, they'd decided all three of them would babysit, as a team. It would give them a chance to see which sitter he clicked with the most, and to look like they were super committed. Plus, they were offering three sitters for the price of one, which his mom, Wendy, would surely appreciate.

127

Wendy had given them the rundown the previous day. They would wait on the front steps until Aloysius's school bus pulled up. Then they would be responsible for him until his mom got home. They had been sitting on the front steps for almost fifteen minutes, and still there was no sign of the bus.

"AHHHH!" Bree screamed out of nowhere. Malia nearly jumped three feet in the air.

Somehow, Aloysius had silently appeared from behind them and tapped Bree on the shoulder. Again, he was wearing all-black clothing, like a child mime. How long had he been home? Where the heck did he come from? How long had he been listening to their conversation? Also, just creepy.

"Aloysius! When did you get home?" Malia asked. "Was your bus early today?"

He just blinked at Malia, with his enormous brown eyes.

"Hi, Aloysius!" Bree said, standing up and opening the front door so they could all go inside. "We're so excited to hang out with you."

The little boy stepped silently through the doorway.

"Does anyone ever call you Al?" Malia asked as they stopped in the entryway to take off their sneakers, adding them to a small row of shoes that were lined up on a little patterned rug.

Aloysius just shook his head.

"How about any other nicknames?" Bree asked.

He just stood there, blinking.

"What do you want to do?" Malia asked.

Blink. Blink.

"Do you have a favorite game?" Bree asked. No response.

"Do you want a snack?" Malia tried. Still nothing. "I know! Let's go play in your room."

He pivoted on one foot and started walking through the house, without a word. Bree and Malia looked at each other, shrugged, and then followed his lead. They followed him down a narrow hallway, into what Malia guessed was his bedroom. The only thing that said "bedroom" was the presence of an actual bed. Beyond that, Aloysius's room was very different than any kid's room Malia had ever seen. It didn't seem like it belonged to a child at all. The decor looked more like the work of a wizard or a historian or a mad professor.

One entire wall was lined with books. There were picture books and board books, as you might expect in a five-year-old's space, but it didn't stop there. There were rows and rows of old-fashioned encyclopedias, classic novels, thick science books and heavy textbooks that looked more complicated than anything she'd encountered, even in middle school. Honestly, it was all pretty intimidating.

Another wall had a giant rack full of medals—the kind you'd get for winning the Olympics or running a marathon. But upon closer inspection, they were all medals for smart-people things: spelling bees, science competitions, math Olympics. Chelsea had a bunch of similar awards at home, but this kid was FIVE, and already he had way more than her.

Next to the medals, there sat a large table that looked like it belonged in a science lab. There were beakers and glass containers, plus rows and rows of plastic bottles, neatly labeled with the names of chemicals. What on earth did a small child need so many chemicals for?

"What's that stuff?" Malia asked, pointing to a huge container full of a mysterious white powder.

"My borax," he said softly, tucking his cheekbone-length dark hair behind one ear.

Right, yes, naturally.

"What do you do with it?" she asked. *Please, kid, just tell me something so we can have a conversation,* Malia thought.

"Science," he said.

Sigh.

"So, what do you feel like doing?" Bree asked.

Aloysius sat down on the ground and crossed his legs. Then he closed his eyes. He sat there, a tiny body forming a tiny lotus position, neither moving nor making a sound.

What the heck? Bree mouthed to Malia. Malia shrugged. Was he meditating? Was this normal? Should they leave him alone?

For a few more moments, they all sat there in silence, as Aloysius visualized himself sitting in a Zen temple, or planning his world takeover, or whatever the heck he was doing. Suddenly, Malia heard the sweet sound of semi-creepy carnival music floating through the open window. The ice cream truck was making its way down the street.

"Aloysius! Would you like some ice cream?" she asked.

His eyes sprang open. "No, thank you," he said, before closing his eyes once more.

"Do you want any kind of treats at all? We're so happy to be here, we'll get you whatever you want!" said Bree.

Aloysius just shook his head.

"Do you want to talk about cats?" Bree pressed on. "Remember? We met yesterday at the cat café. I love cats." No response from Aloysius. "I have a cat named Taylor Swift after, you know, Taylor Swift." No response. "She's my favorite.

Sometimes when she's in my room, we act out scenes from *Cats* the musical."

"You do?!" Malia said. She knew Bree was a lover of all cheesy musicals, but this was news to her. Malia would've happily paid, like, all of the money she didn't have to see that.

"Yes," Bree responded, somewhat defensively.

"I bet Aloysius would love to see you perform something from *Cats*. Wouldn't you, Aloysius?"

He opened his right eye, just a smidge. After a moment, he opened the other. "I guess that might be entertaining," he admitted. Jackpot.

Bree shot Malia a look that let her know she was not amused. But this was an important job, and they needed to make this little boy happy. And so, within a matter of moments, Bree crouched down on all fours and mimed licking her paws.

"Okay, so this song is about Mr. Mistoffelees," she said.

"WHO?" Malia asked.

"He's, like, one of the most important cats in the show. He has the best dance." She cleared her throat. And then she was off. *"OH, WELL, I NEVER, WAS THERE EVER A CAT SO CLEVER AS MAGICAL MR. MISTOFFELEES,"* sang Bree as she twirled in crazy circles. It was an epic performance. She kicked her legs even higher than her head and swung her arms around and made jazz hands. For the grand finale, she leaped several feet in the air and somehow landed on all fours, like a cat.

Aloysius watched her curiously the entire time she was dancing. At one point, he almost cracked a smile. Malia didn't know how he wasn't laughing hysterically, because Bree's cat dance was quite possibly the best thing Malia had ever, ever seen. By the time Bree finished, Malia was laughing so hard she couldn't breathe.

"Bree! Your moves! I had no idea you could dance like that."

"Well, I just really like cats," she said with a shrug.

They looked back at Aloysius. He had reclosed his eyes and was back to sitting perfectly still, like a seasoned meditator. If he had been in the yard, they may have mistaken him for a lawn statue.

Malia started typing wildly into her phone.

"What are you doing?" asked Bree.

"Calling in backup," Malia said.

CHAPTER SEVENTEEN

Dot

By the time Dot arrived at Aloysius's house, she was quite frankly scared to go inside. In the time it took for her science fair meeting to wrap up, Malia's text messages had gone from *Where are you??* to *Help! It doesn't speak* to *S.O.S. Bring ice cream. Bring candy. Bring whatever you think a child will like.*

You sure? Dot typed back. *Remember what happened to the Woo kids with too much sugar.*

Yes, came her certain response. *Trust me on this one. Must bribe.*

Even though Dot thought such bribery was likely unnecessary, no one had to tell her twice to pack junk food. So she rummaged around in her locker's personal snack supply and arrived armed with a backpack full of candy. And three different flavors of potato chips, "borrowed" from the school cafeteria's snack bar, just in case she—rather, the child—was in the mood for something savory.

"We're in here!" called Malia once Dot had closed the front door. Dot followed the sound of Malia's voice down a hallway until she found them. The scene Dot encountered wasn't the bedlam she expected, but it was still plenty weird. Everyone was sitting on the floor, legs crossed beneath them, in total silence. It looked like one of her mom's silent Buddhist retreats.

"Hello!" she said, prompting everyone but Aloysius to come to life. "I'm so sorry I'm late. Science waits for no one." She dropped the freakishly heavy snack bag onto the floor.

"How was your meeting?" asked Bree.

"It was good! I mean, there's no better way to end one's day than discussing bacteria and how it responds to music."

"Bacteria? What kind of bacteria?" Aloysius exclaimed before Dot had a chance to finish. "What kind of music?" His entire face brightened, and his eyes grew huge and sparkly and alive, like the alarmingly oversize eyes of a Disney princess.

"It speaks," whispered Malia, so low Dot could barely hear her.

"I'm working on a project for the middle school science

fair, about whether bacteria has a preference for different types of music," Dot explained. "So I'm growing three different samples of bacteria—all collected from the same gross place on the school drinking fountain—and exposing each one to a different type of music: classical, the Beatles, and Taylor Swift."

"That is so gross," said Malia.

"Taylor Swift?" asked Bree.

"When did you collect the samples? Are you growing them in identical environments? Is there a control sample that isn't listening to any music? How has the growth been so far? How often are you tracking and recording it? Does it seem like one genre has a considerable lead?" Aloysius was a veritable fountain of questions.

"WHAT ARE YOU GUYS TALKING ABOUT?" Malia grumbled.

Dot sighed. "Aloysius is just showing a genuine interest in my project."

"Right. Cool. We're going to go tear into these snacks. You guys want anything?" Malia asked, snatching up the bag. Dot barely had time to respond before Malia and Bree made a beeline for the door and disappeared from sight.

"So, it looks like you have a lot of your own experiments

going on in here, huh?" Dot asked as she surveyed the room. It reminded her a little bit of her own room when she was his age.

"Yes!" He wandered over to the bookshelf and started pulling volumes off it. "Right now I'm working on a few things to test the nature of ionic and covalent bonds," he said casually, like that wasn't something better suited for a high school student. "Sometimes I find ideas for experiments from the Internet, but lately I've been reading some of these really great textbooks my mom found for sale in our old town. None of my classmates can really read yet—like at all—and it can be frustrating to feel like I have no one to connect with."

Dot understood that feeling well. In fact, she had felt the same for pretty much her entire time at school. She would often find herself getting ahead of course work, and she used to sneak more advanced books into class and place them on her lap or in her desk so she could occupy herself while the rest of the class moved at a slower pace.

"Would you want to check out any of these?" Aloysius asked, spreading a bunch of books out on the floor.

"Yes!" Dot said. "I would love that!" In a weird way, she felt like she actually had a lot to learn from this little boy.

Dot gave him the full update on her science fair project:

where she got the idea, how often she was charting the progress, and how the bacteria showed a distinct distaste for Taylor Swift. Malia and Bree had filed back into the room and sat nearby, silently consuming gummy worms.

"What kind of bacteria wouldn't like Taylor Swift?" asked Bree, who seemed personally insulted by the news.

"How's it going in here?" came an adult voice. Wendy appeared in the doorway, wearing a long black dress.

"Mom, Dot's currently working on an experiment about bacteria listening to music!" Aloysius exclaimed.

"That's wonderful, sweetie. I'm so glad you had things to talk about." She beamed. Then, to Dot, she added, "It seems like you've all had a nice afternoon."

"It was a pleasure," Dot said, and meant it. This job had magically exceeded all of her admittedly low expectations.

"So, we'll see you again tomorrow?" Malia asked. After all, this was supposed to be a regular after-school gig.

"Oh, not tomorrow," Wendy said, a wrinkle forming in her brow. "Aloysius will be attending a mini Mensa after-school program for the next couple weeks."

"The next . . . couple weeks?" Malia said.

"Yes. The program starts tomorrow, and runs through the

fall break. We'd still love to hire you for regular sitting, just as soon as his program is through."

Dot inhaled sharply. The fall break was when they needed the deposit for the venue. They had exactly two weeks to earn it, and now there was no chance this job would help them reach their goal.

Dot looked at Malia. She looked back at Dot. Bree just stared at the floor.

"Of course we'll be here as soon as he's back!" Dot said. It wasn't great timing, but a job was still a job. And against all odds, she'd actually enjoyed this one.

CHAPTER EIGHTEEN

MALIA-BECAUSE-CLEARLY-NOBODY-IS-GOING-TO-SAY-ALIA-SO-WHATEVER

Before starting the club, Malia had no idea that running a business was going to be so hard. There were so many things to consider—rates, competition, customer service, not to mention finding actual customers in the first place. Then you had to factor in their schedules and their special after-school programs. Last but not least, there was the hardest job of all: preventing your evil sister from stealing your clients out from under you.

As soon as Malia got home from watching Aloysius, she trudged into the kitchen to find Chelsea sitting at the table, typing away on her laptop, next to a platter of chips and guac. Was nowhere safe?

"Malia!" Chelsea said in a super-friendly tone, as if they actually liked each other. They never addressed each other that way. Malia was immediately suspicious.

"How are you, younger sibling?" Chelsea asked in the same singsong voice. She seemed even gloatier than usual, which was really saying something for a person who practically floated through life on a cloud of her own accomplishments.

"What do you want, witch monster?" Malia asked.

"You know, Malia, if I were you, I would really reexamine the way we relate to each other. I could be a wonderful resource for you."

"I don't need a resource, but thanks for the offer."

"I'm just saying, I excel in all areas—academics, extracurricular, social—and now business. And you could obviously benefit from some guidance."

"DO YOU EVEN HAVE A SOUL?" Malia yelled.

"Malia, we're just having a conversation. There's no need to raise your voice."

"I wasn't raising my voice," Malia said, even though she obviously was.

"Most people would probably kill for a sister like me, to lead the way and then share her secrets."

"But you don't share anything. Not even the guacamole," Malia said, gesturing to the table.

"Would you like some guacamole?"

"No! But if I did, you probably wouldn't share it. You'd say it was, like, winner's guacamole and I wasn't capable of eating it. Or something."

"Well, I do tend to win at everything. But I would still share the guacamole with you." She smiled sweetly.

"What are you getting at?" Malia asked.

"Running a successful business is so easy, and so profitable, and is just one more thing that's going to look really good on college applications. And now I can say I've run an *award-winning* business."

"What do you mean?" Malia asked.

She casually slid a magazine across the table. It was the latest copy of *What'sUp, Playa del Mar,* the magazine read by everyone in town. Malia saw it was already open to a spread featuring photos of Chelsea and her terrible Seaside friends, smiling and hanging out with children. Malia picked it up to get a closer look, which is when she realized her hands were shaking.

Three local teens decided to get entrepreneurial by starting a babysitting business, the aptly named Seaside Sitters. In just a

matter of weeks, they've turned an incredible profit, made a dif-
ference in countless children's lives, and unified a community in the
process.

"One day, the idea just came to us," said the group's vice
president and marketing director, Camilla Jenson-Lee. "It's as if
this was destined to happen."

"It's been one incredible ride, but the best is yet to come,"
said chief executive officer Chelsea Twiggs, referring to one epic
upcoming job, in which they'll be tasked with watching thirty-three
children at a local family's reunion.

The teens, especially Twiggs, are no strangers to impressive
résumés. Twiggs maintains a perfect 4.0 GPA, is a member of
the National Honor Society, and is the president of her class at
Playa del Mar High School.

"What the . . ." Malia took a second to process what she
had just seen. "This isn't fair. You stole our idea! Then you
stole all our clients! This entire thing is built on lies!" Malia
shook the magazine above her head. She was so angry, her entire body was vibrating

"That's not really fair, little sister. Everyone has known
about babysitting clubs since the height of their popular-
ity in the 1980s. How many classic horror movies involved

someone calling a babysitter? It's what they call public domain."

"I'm not talking about horror movies! I'm talking about my life!" Malia shouted.

"It's not personal, Malia, it's just business. There's no need to get so worked up about it."

"But . . . but . . . you've already taken all the business in town. You could at least give us credit for having the idea!"

"Tell that to the thirty-three kids we'll be watching at the Larssons' family reunion. Your little idea doesn't matter when our execution is perfect. Also, we're getting paid our usual rates *per child*."

"YOU HORRIBLE THING!" Malia yelled. She couldn't help it. It just burst out of her.

"Malia! That's no way to speak to your sister." Her mother appeared in the doorway.

Malia threw her hands up in the air. "That's not fair! Chelsea was being mean. You didn't hear the first part of that conversation."

"I didn't have to. No matter what, you shouldn't be calling each other names. You know I won't tolerate name-calling in this house."

"But Chelsea lied!" Malia yelled.

"She's just jealous." Chelsea rolled her eyes.

"Malia, did you congratulate your sister on her magazine feature? It really is impressive."

"YAAAAAAARRRRRRRRRRRRRRRRG!" Malia yelled as she turned and stomped out of the kitchen.

"Malia, do not storm out that way! And don't stomp your feet," her mom called. But Malia could barely hear her. She was already in her room, with the door closed behind her. This was completely unfair. She didn't even care about the money anymore. She didn't even care about the party. Those things would be nice, for sure, but this was about good versus evil. This was about . . . revenge.

CHAPTER NINETEEN

Dot

Ding *dong the witch is going down in flames,* read the latest group text Malia sent to Bree and Dot. The witch in question was Chelsea, and Malia had sent many similar texts all morning, in preparation for their next club meeting. Apparently Malia had hatched a brilliant plan to sabotage Seaside once and for all, and everyone was headed to Malia's house to hear all about it. Ever since the job at Aloysius's house, tensions had been high, as all three girls seemed annoyed with Seaside, the looming deadline to come up with a deposit, and, on some level, each other.

Should I bring snacks? texted Bree.

Obviously, Dot replied.

Adios, witch! texted Malia.

Dot grabbed her backpack, gave her room a quick scan to

make sure all contraband bath and body products were safely out of sight, and set off.

Just as she was making her way through the living room, her mom burst through the front door.

"My little Dot! What's new in your world? I feel like I've barely seen you," she said, making her way over to Dot and combing her fingers through Dot's hair.

"I'm on my way to Malia's. Apparently there's another babysitting-related crisis we need to address."

"I see. How about we catch up for a minute. Do you want to do a quick rune reading?" she asked. "Sometimes a little insight can be particularly helpful in moments of crisis."

Runes were another of her mom's "special" divination tools, along with tarot cards, tea leaves, and pendulums. Essentially, they were little stones with symbols carved into them. You pulled them out of a bag, and the symbols helped give you insight into whatever was going on in your life.

"I mean, I'm not having a crisis," Dot said, with a shrug. "Malia is just being dramatic. You know her."

"Still, a little insight never hurt anyone, hmm?" she said.

They both took a seat on the purple sofa. Her mom held out the little velvet pouch, and Dot reached her hand into it. Her fingers found their way around a smooth, cool stone, and she pulled it out so they could see which one it was. The symbol looked kind of like a pointy letter *P*. Her mom scrunched up her face and made a "huh" sound, like whatever she'd discovered was surprising.

"So, what does that mean?" Dot asked. Crisis or not, she wasn't particularly in the mood for a bad omen.

"Well, this is the symbol for *Purisaz*," she said, pointing to the little gold character etched into the stone.

"And . . ." Sometimes her mom had a tendency to forget that Dot didn't have all of her mom's bizarre New Agery committed to memory, even though she'd been forcing it on Dot since she was a zygote.

"Well, *Purisaz* can sometimes mean that you have a choice in front of you. You may need to make a decision that will cause something to change. And often, it seems like things will get much worse before they can get better."

"Well, that's grim." She couldn't really think of anything that would require making a choice. Still, leave it to Dot's mom to take an otherwise lovely afternoon to a weird, dark place.

"Does that remind you of anything going on in your life right now?" she asked. "What's this crisis you were referring to?"

Dot let out a deep breath. "Eh, it isn't really a crisis. Malia's sister made her own babysitters thing called the Seaside Sitters, and they're being sort of annoying, trying to take all the business in town. We started the club to help pay for our group birthday party and also to get paid for hanging out, but now . . . well, it seems kind of doomed."

Her mom just listened and nodded in all the right places.

"Well, Dot, I'm glad to hear you're in good spirits. But whatever you do, whatever choices you make, consider karma," she advised. "What you put out into the world has energy. If you make choices from a place of loving kindness, and try to honor what's in your heart while doing no harm to others, you can't go wrong."

Dot nodded her head. It sounded nice, in theory, but it didn't feel particularly relevant to what was going on with her or her friends or the club. Plus, sometimes it was hard to do the right thing in everyday life. There were so many factors to consider. She didn't know what Malia had up her sleeve, but when it came to Chelsea, it hardly ever stemmed from a place of loving kindness.

"Choices aren't bad, Dot," her mom said, holding the rune up one last time before placing it back in the velvet pouch.

"Neither is change. I sense that some changes might be coming your way. Remember, never be afraid to follow your inner compass."

"We're going to destroy Seaside!" Malia said, slamming her fist down onto her desk with so much force that everything in her room gave a little wobble.

Dot couldn't help but note that, from a karmic perspective, this did not sound very positive.

"I've been spying," Malia continued. "Yesterday afternoon, I pretended to feel sick so I could come home from school early. Then I looked through Chelsea's desk. And her computer. And maybe also her drawers, just for fun. Anyway. Seaside is *completely* booked this weekend—all three of them have jobs that take up, like, all of the hours—so I thought it might be fun to hire them for *another* job that's too good to pass up, just to make things interesting."

"I don't get it." Bree scratched her ankle. "If they're already booked, why would they take another job?"

"And why would *we* hire them?" Dot asked.

"So, this job—a totally fake job that I made up—is for Mrs. Abernathy. You know that house that's so enormous it looks like the White House? She's a super-rich lady who would pay big money to have someone watch her super-fancy children. I know Chelsea, and I knew she wouldn't be able to pass it up. This is everything she lives for. So I made a fake email account and I wrote her this email."

Malia cleared her throat and began reading in a high, snooty voice.

"Dear Ms. Chelsea Twiggs, I hope this electronic correspondence finds you well. My name is Ramona Abernathy. I live in the stately Georgian home on Robles Street. You know, the one with the giant columns that looks like a government building? You've likely noticed it, since it's the largest home in the entire county and has been featured in many books of a historical nature. Anyhow, I find myself in need of quality sittery—"

"Sittery isn't a word," Dot interrupted. Malia rolled her eyes and kept on reading.

"Once again—*I find myself in need of quality sittery for this coming weekend. I will have a home full of grandchildren and am prepared to pay you a very large sum. I will require your presence for the entire afternoon, and I am requesting you specifically, since your credentials are the most impressive of any sitter I've ever heard of, anywhere, ever. Please RSVP to this email as soon as possible. Sincerely, Ramona Abernathy."*

Malia paused for dramatic effect. She was beaming.

"So then what happened?" Bree was rapt. It was like she was watching a TV drama and couldn't wait for the next plot point to unfold.

"Well, Chelsea immediately responded to the email and said she'd be there. I knew she would. She's so predictable sometimes. Mrs. Abernathy is a retired tech mogul and is super well respected or famous or whatever and that's exactly the kind of person Chelsea loves to kiss up to."

"I'm still not sure I follow," Dot said.

"Well, accepting the job with Mrs. Abernathy meant she needed to cancel the job she'd already booked." Malia stopped to let out a delighted giggle. "Of course she would never just cancel, because that would make her look bad. So she asked if I would step in for her. And that's how I booked a job for Saturday, with the delightful Albert family."

"You're like an evil genius," said Bree.

"But what's going to happen when she goes to Mrs. Abernathy's house and discovers the job is fake?" Dot asked. This plan might be creative, but it definitely had its flaws. Plus, even when dealing with someone as evil as Chelsea, it wasn't right to flat-out lie.

"I don't know. She embarrasses herself in front of a person

she'd actually want to impress? And she finally gets a taste of her own medicine."

"What if she somehow figures out you're the one who wrote the fake email?" Dot pressed on.

"She'll never be able to prove it."

Despite the many, many ways in which this seemed like a bad idea, Malia seemed absolutely set on this plan going forward. Dot tried to consult her internal compass, but it just felt like it was spinning in circles. She had no idea which direction was right.

CHAPTER TWENTY

MALIA

BUT MOM ALWAYS LETS US SCOOT IN THE STREET!" yelled Christopher, Malia's seven-year-old babysitting charge, who was practically having a meltdown while perched on his blue scooter.

"YEAH! WHAT HE SAID!" yelled Caroline, his fraternal twin sister.

Malia was more than halfway through her semi-stolen babysitting job, and so far, so good. She was pretty sure the twins kept trying to pull one over on her—so far they had told her their mother let them eat ice cream all day, had given them permission to adopt a kitten, let them watch whatever TV shows they wanted regardless of the maturity rating, and let them ride their scooters in the street. She had met their very overprotective mother, and you didn't need to be a rocket scientist to know that none of this was true.

"Well, as you may have noticed, I am clearly not your mother," Malia said. "And I am not interested in letting you play out in the street today. Scooting on the sidewalk can be fun, too. And it's way less dangerous."

"Incorrect. It's not fun at all." Christopher crossed his arms defiantly.

"Not even a little fun," added Caroline.

"I have an idea. How about you guys race each other?"

"In the street?" asked Christopher.

Malia sighed. "No. On the sidewalk. One of you can take this side, and one of you can take the sidewalk across the street. First person to reach the stop sign on the corner wins ice cream. But absolutely no scooting into the street, or else you're disqualified."

Their eyes lit up, and they were off. Malia had to admit that babysitting was continuing to grow on her. At home, she never won an argument, never got to come out on top. But with babysitting, she was the one in charge, and she thought she was pretty good at it.

"I'm coming for you!" yelled Christopher.

"Eat my dust, loser!" yelled Caroline.

Malia momentarily wondered if there were any siblings out there who actually enjoyed each other's company.

The twins were insanely competitive, and one race quickly turned into best out of three, followed by best out of five. An hour of scooting breezed right by, without either of them ever venturing into the street.

Mrs. Albert returned home to two happy children, and she seemed very pleased. Malia was equally pleased when she was handed a stack of twenty-dollar bills.

As Malia walked home from the job, she felt proud of herself. Pride was a weird, unfamiliar feeling, and she realized with horror that it might be the first time she'd ever felt that way.

Miraculously, her plan to sabotage Chelsea had worked! The job watching the Albert kids had gone well. And best of all, she'd gotten paid! They were one step closer to having party funds, which made them one step closer to an actual party.

Today, Malia thought, *was the day Malia Twiggs finally won.* She was in the mood to celebrate.

Anything new? Malia texted Dot and Bree.

Still nothing, Dot answered.

Since they were afraid of something going horribly wrong with Chelsea's fake job, Dot and Bree had hidden in the bushes on the Abernathy estate. That way, they would be the first to know if a furious Chelsea was coming to enact revenge. So far, though, there was nothing to report.

Apparently Chelsea arrived on time (of course; according to her, punctuality was a virtue), and went inside the house, but never left. It was curious, to say the least. Did she get talked into watering plants or helping out around the house? What if she got in trouble for trespassing? What if she was being held prisoner? Malia thought about it for a second. If Chelsea got abducted, her mom would probably be really mad, like the maddest Malia had ever seen her. But ultimately, some Chelsea-free time wouldn't be so bad . . .

Giving up, Dot texted. *She's still here. Don't know what happened, but this shrub is getting itchy.*

OK. Good effort, Malia answered.

She took the long way home, stopping at the Playa del Market to pick up a celebratory chocolate bar. Whatever had happened to Chelsea, the day was still a success. She took a bite of it as she rounded the corner onto her street. She felt like nothing could stop her.

"Malia!"

And then something stopped her. Malia looked up to see Chelsea, standing in their driveway, which meant she was not locked up somewhere in Mrs. Abernathy's house. She also appeared to be . . . happy. How could this be?

"Oh, little sister. Today, the most wonderful thing happened — something every wildly successful person dreams of."

"You evaded paying taxes?" Malia guessed. She didn't even know what that meant, but it seemed like people on the news were always talking about that.

"I found a mentor."

"What?" Malia said. This was unexpected.

"It's honestly a miracle. There's no other way to explain it. I received an email from some bogus account asking me to meet with Mrs. Abernathy. You know her, right? She used to be at the helm of one of the companies hailed for changing the face of the Internet. She lives in the biggest house I've ever seen."

Malia just stood there, her jaw hanging open, as Chelsea went on and on. Apparently Mrs. Abernathy was so impressed with Chelsea that she invited her inside for tea and they bonded over what Malia could only imagine was their mutual appreciation for being really, really uptight.

"She's going to teach me *everything,* Malia. Coding. Search engine optimization. Negotiation. How to run a company. How to win friends and influence people! Plus, she said she'll write personal recommendations for my college applications! Do you know how valuable that is? Now I can basically write my ticket to anywhere I want to go!" She laughed a sinister laugh. She would probably say it wasn't a sinister laugh, but it definitely was. "I'm practically unstoppable now! Today is the best day I have EVER had."

Malia was speechless. Chelsea was like one of Bree's beloved cats; she had nine lives and was always somehow able to land on her feet. How was it possible?

"Wow, that's . . . that's something," Malia choked out. "I'm really happy for you." She turned and attempted to scurry into the house as fast as she could. The whole interaction had left her feeling deflated, and she had to escape before things could possibly get any worse. Unfortunately, Chelsea followed close behind her.

"How did the babysitting job go?" she asked.

"It was good! The kids were really nice. Their mom was happy. So glad everything worked out," Malia called over her shoulder, making a beeline for the front steps.

"So I'll need two-thirds of the fee," Chelsea said.

Malia stopped in her tracks.

"Excuse me?"

"Well, it was technically my job. They hired the Seaside Sitters, not you. You never would have found that job without me. So I'm entitled to a referral fee."

"Two-thirds? TWO-THIRDS? How is that a referral fee? That's, like, more than half of the money!"

"Yes, two-thirds is more than half. Glad you understand fractions, Malia."

"You didn't tell me about this beforehand! How can you spring this on me now?"

"It's pretty common sense. In fact, I think it's really nice that I'm letting you keep ANY of the money."

"How dare you! I earned that money! This is why I would never ever do you a favor! This is why I will NEVER do anything nice for you EVER again!"

Malia's mom stuck her head out the front door. "What on earth is going on out here? If you two are going to yell, can you at least take it inside? You're causing a scene!"

The sisters angrily filed into the house.

"Now, who wants to tell me what's going on here?" their mom asked.

Chelsea started speaking before Malia could even open her mouth.

"Malia filled in for a Seaside Sitters job today. It was

technically my job, and was booked through me. Malia offered to fill in as a favor, and I thought that was a wonderful idea. You know how I'm invested in her development, and it seemed like an excellent learning opportunity for her. I've simply requested a small referral fee, for finding her the job—which I find to be quite generous of me—and she started calling me terrible names."

"That is NOT what happened!" Malia snapped.

"Malia, it's nice that your sister is letting you participate in her business and very generous of her to let you keep the money as well."

Chelsea gloated.

"But that's not—"

"I don't want to hear any more about this. There's enough tumult in the world right now without two sisters getting upset with each other over money."

Her mom glared at Malia, then turned to leave the room. Malia tried to think of something—anything—to say to make it better. But as usual, she felt so flustered that she couldn't find the right words. Chelsea just smirked, then flounced away. Would it ever end? She stole Malia's idea, she stole her business, and now she had stolen her pride.

CHAPTER TWENTY-ONE

Bree

*B*AM *BAM BAM BAM BAM BAM BAM BAM!*

Marc and Bree's mom were sprawled out on the living room carpet, playing a game of Hungry Hungry Hippos with Emma and Bailey. It was part of some new kick her mom was on where everyone was supposed to play with "analog" things to spend less time staring at their phones and stuff. Last week had been puzzle week, but Olivia had eaten one of the little cardboard pieces, and that was the end of puzzle week. This week was game week.

Now there was a lot of banging and a lot of plastic marbles flying everywhere. Olivia sat nearby—safely out of reach of the marbles—shouting "HIPPO!" every twenty seconds.

"Everyone. My friends are coming over!" Bree announced.

"That's great, Bree," said her mom, concentrating on her hippo.

"We're going to be discussing some very top secret things, so unfortunately I don't think there will be much time to spend with you guys."

"Hippo!" said Olivia. Nobody else responded.

"YES!" Marc yelled, the same way he did whenever basketball was on TV. Bree guessed his hippo did something impressive.

"Oh, you show-off," said Mom.

"HIPPOOOOO!" screeched Olivia.

"All right, well, I guess I'll check in with you later," Bree said. Still, nobody replied. "Bye!" she yelled for good measure.

Then she headed to her room to wait for Malia and Dot to arrive. Bree loved her family, and she loved her cat, and she loved her room. Really, she loved everything about her life. Sometimes, though, she felt like her friends were the only people in the world who noticed she was alive. Bree really didn't know what she'd do without them.

Malia arrived first, and before she even had a chance to say anything, Bree could tell something was wrong.

"I don't want to talk about it until Dot gets here," she said. "I don't think I can bear to tell the story twice."

Instead, Malia helped Bree carry tons of snacks up from the kitchen and spread them out all over the floor.

"Are you excited? Your birthday is coming up soon," Malia said.

"Of course!" Bree said. Because obvi. Birthdays are the most exciting. They're holidays just for you. "But I'm even more excited for fall break, and for the party! I don't think it will really feel like my birthday has happened until we can all celebrate together." It was true. This was the first year Bree was even more excited about their joint birthday than her actual day.

Dot arrived a minute later and immediately started digging into the snacks. That's when Malia told them what had happened with Chelsea—how she and old Mrs. Abernathy had somehow become friends, and how Chelsea demanded two-thirds of the money Malia had earned for babysitting. Bree had seen Malia be angry at Chelsea before, but this was different. She seemed super sad, like her old beta fish had when it got this weird scale disease and couldn't do anything except kind of float around slowly in its bowl, looking depressed.

"You guys, I can't believe I'm about to say this, but—"

Before Malia could finish her sentence, the door flew open and Olivia exploded through it.

"Bweeeeeeee!" Olivia toddled into the center of the room at warp speed. She threw her arms around Bree's neck and started hugging her so hard it felt like she might want to kill Bree.

"Hi, Olivia," Bree said.

"It's sweet how much she loves you," Malia said. "I've honestly never hugged my sister on purpose."

"Siblings. Weird," said Dot.

"Where cat?" Olivia asked.

"I don't know," Bree said, slightly hurt that it seemed she'd only come here to find the cat.

"No Puddin'?"

"No. Taylor Swift is not here," Bree responded. "I don't know where *Taylor Swift* is."

"PUDDIN'!" Olivia yelled.

"Taylor Swift," Bree corrected.

"PUDDIN'!" she called as she toddled off through the doorway. "PUDDIN' PUDDIN' PUDDIN'!"

"Well, that was interesting," said Dot.

"It seems like your cat name rebrand is going about as well as mine is," said Malia-who-they-kept-forgetting-to-call-Alia.

"Look, what I was about to say before is that I'm tired of playing by the rules. The rules haven't gotten me anywhere."

"You've broken into your sister's personal electronics, sent her bogus emails from made-up accounts, and recently sent her on a fake babysitting job. I think, technically, that's not really playing by the rules," Dot said.

"Whatever! More rules must be broken."

"What kind of rules?" asked Dot, her eyes suddenly as wide as the king-size peanut butter cups she kept putting in her mouth.

"We're going to take down Seaside once and for all. By proving they're not as good as they claim they are."

"But . . . how do we do that?" Bree asked.

"By catching them in the act, and recording it. We need photos, videos, interviews, anything we can find."

"You mean—" Dot honestly looked more excited than Bree had ever seen her. "We're going to spy?"

Malia just nodded.

"Like, with gear and stuff?"

"Yes. We can wear camouflage and crawl around on the ground and swing from ropes! Or maybe we can just listen to conversations through the wall using a drinking glass. I don't know. We'll figure it out."

"Oh my goodness!" said Bree.

"We should watch some spy movies for inspiration," said Dot.

"Where do we get camouflage?" asked Bree. "Where do we get ropes?" She clapped her hands together. Babysitting was so much weirder than she ever expected! Bree had been thrilled just to be part of a club, but this was turning out to be all kinds of fun.

CHAPTER TWENTY-TWO

Dot

Dot was sure it wasn't what her mom would classify as good karma, but she was pretty excited about spying. Playa del Mar was the kind of town where nothing interesting happened—like once there was an unusually large raccoon running around eating people's trash, and that made it onto the front page of the paper. So until Dot was closer to realizing her dreams of moving to a real city, she would have to settle for excitement wherever she could find it. And this was the most exciting thing they had come up with, well, ever.

The plan was to gather at Malia's house, wearing all-black clothing. *Like a ninja,* Malia's text read. Dot wasn't sure if the spy wear was absolutely necessary, but she supposed it couldn't hurt. Plus, she really only wore black, anyway.

When the three of them actually convened, though, they

looked like they were on their way to a séance or a funeral, or in Bree's case, a black-tie affair. She was wearing a glittery black cocktail dress, which Dot recognized as part of the previous year's Halloween costume, paired with black socks and black combat boots. Rounding out the look was a GoPro camera strapped to her forehead.

"*That's* your spy outfit?" Malia said.

"It's black. You said to wear black, did you not?"

"Bree! Glitter is highly visible," Malia said. "Even when it's black."

"Well, this is the only black outfit I own."

"You could have borrowed something," Dot offered.

She just shrugged. "Still works."

"Where'd you get a GoPro?" Dot asked.

"It's Marc's. He uses it to make videos of himself surfing or something."

Naturally.

"Okay, so, like, how do you spy?" asked Bree.

"The better question is: What are our objectives?" Dot said. "What are the things we're hoping to get out of this?"

"I want to uncover every horrible thing they do on the job," said Malia. "Do they sneak boyfriends into the house during babysitting jobs? Steal things? Ignore the kids? They don't speak Dutch, but somehow they're teaching it! Something is amiss, and we're going to find out exactly what it is."

Dot had to hand it to Malia—she had really thought this one through. She was shaping up to be a pretty impressive CEO, in more ways than one. Malia thrust papers into each of their hands.

"Here are copies of all three sitters' schedules for today, along with any relevant addresses, names, and important things to watch out for. Our task is to divide and conquer. Each of us will follow one sitter through her entire job. I want footage at every stage of the babysitting gig, from beginning to end. Do whatever you need to do in order to get it. I repeat: DO WHATEVER IT TAKES. Just don't get caught."

They nodded confidently. Dot resisted the urge to salute. And then they were off.

Malia was spying on Chelsea, of course. Bree was following Camilla. This meant Dot was tasked with following Sidney, who was babysitting for the Woo girls. Luckily, Dot was already familiar with the Woos' house, which made her job easier. She knew exactly where all the prime windows were, including which were located near bushes for her to hide in.

The living room window was already open a crack, so she could record audio footage in addition to visual.

As soon as Mrs. Woo left the house, Sidney settled onto the floor with the kids. Ruby carried a puzzle box into the room, and they dumped the pieces onto the ground. Then the three of them—Ruby, Jemima, and Sidney—sat on the floor, silently working on the jigsaw puzzle. It was so peaceful and bizarrely picturesque, it looked like something right off the Seaside Sitters website. Dot had spent time with these girls before, and she didn't know they were capable of silence. What was Seaside's secret?

Dot watched this scene unfold for another few minutes. At one point, Jemima toddled off toward the kitchen, and Dot was hopeful that meant some disaster was about to ensue. Instead, she came back with three sticks of string cheese. The trio quietly ate the cheese while working on the puzzle. This was officially shaping up to be the worst spy mission ever.

"I wanna play beauty parlor!" said Ruby.

"Yes, yes! Pahh-lahh," parroted Jemima.

"Um, okay. You guys can do whatever you want. Just do it quietly and don't make a mess, okay?" said Sidney. She pulled a small bag out of her purse and started doing her makeup. A very angsty Ruby climbed to her feet and stood beside her.

"Hey! Why are YOU playing beauty parlor on yourself?" asked Ruby, grabbing one of Sidney's compacts off the floor.

"Hey, put that down. That's not for you," Sidney snapped.

"LADY! PAY ATTENTION TO ME!" Ruby yelled.

"Don't be a brat," said Sidney.

"I WANNA PLAY BEAUTY PARLOR!" Ruby shrieked.

"PLAY PAHHHH-LAHHHH!" yelled Jemima.

"Just watch TV, okay?"

"NO! I'm the haircutter and I want to trim your bangs!" Ruby crossed her small arms angrily across her chest.

"Do you really have to talk so loud?" Sidney rolled her eyes.

"I'M GONNA DYE YOUR HAIR BLUE BECAUSE I HATE YOU!"

It went on this way for far too long. Dot dutifully recorded the entire episode, but it took every ounce of self-control for her to not intervene. The Woo girls could be kind of high-strung, even a little insane, but still. Seeing the kids this upset kind of broke her heart.

"JACKSON! HOW'S IT GOING OUT THERE?" Sidney screamed. Was she yelling out for a boyfriend? Dot looked across the front lawn toward the open garage door, where a scrawny little kid poked his head out from behind the Woos' Jeep. She recognized him as one of the weird kindergarten boys who liked to play near the gazebo.

Something about this scenario seemed very weird. Jackpot.

"I'm going as fast as I can, Sidney!" he called out. He seemed like he was on the verge of hyperventilating. From her spot in the bushes, Dot only had a partial view of the garage. But she needed to find out more. Was this situation possibly what it looked like? Had the Seaside Sitters actually hired this small child to clean for them?

Dot crawled out from behind the bush and brushed the random twigs and leaves off her clothing. She headed toward the Woos' garage, trying to assume the posture of a random kid taking a stroll through the neighborhood. She had to get the whole story from Jackson.

"Hi there!" Dot waved at him. "Whatcha doing?"

"Um, cleaning this garage," he said. "And raking leaves. And doing yard work."

"Cool! That's so nice of you," Dot said. "Do you live here? Are they paying you to do that?"

"Some lady found me at the playground this morning and said if I helped her out, she would buy me candy."

"I hope it's a lot of candy," said Dot.

"A Take 5," said Jackson matter-of-factly.

"Just one candy bar? You must really like them," Dot said.

"Yeah. They're pretty good," he said with a shrug. "Well, I better get back to work or she's going to be mad." He pointed back at the house.

Wow. So the Seaside Sitters weren't magical garage organizers, after all. They were con artists. Dot couldn't wait to share her findings with Bree and Malia. But her work here wasn't done. She crept back to a nearby bush to record some video footage of poor Jackson performing manual labor.

She had only been there for a few minutes when she heard a disturbing sound. It was like someone had turned on a giant faucet. Dot realized exactly what was happening a moment too late. The automatic sprinkler system had turned on, with her in the middle of it. She slipped her phone into her backpack before it could get drenched, but her clothes were not as fortunate.

Dot was so keyed up that she ran all the way back to Malia's. By the time she got there, she was almost dry.

As soon as they saw one another, all three of the girls broke out into some semblance of, "OH MY GOD, YOU GUYS, LOOK WHAT I GOT!"

"I can't wait for you both to see this!" Dot said, brandishing her phone.

"No, seriously, you're not going to believe this," said Bree.

"You guys, I was so scared at one point that I almost peed," said Malia. Bree and Dot regarded her with disgusted looks. "Don't look at me like that, I said *almost*. I didn't actually pee. It's, like, a figure of speech or whatever."

Bree and Dot continued to regard her curiously.

"Whatever. Look what I got!" She proceeded to show them video footage of Chelsea "minding" the Larsson triplets in a very terrible way. Camilla's boyfriend Danny had, in fact, paid her a visit at her babysitting job. And of course, Dot shared her footage of Sidney yelling at the cute little Woo girls. Collectively, they had compiled *hours* of evidence to make their case. Now it was just a matter of editing it down and sharing it with the world.

They were so engrossed in the footage that they didn't notice Chelsea poke her head through the door.

"What are you weirdos doing?" she asked just as Malia shoved her phone under a pillow.

"Nothing, big sister." Malia smiled sweetly. As soon as Chelsea was gone, she added, "Just ruining your life."

CHAPTER TWENTY-THREE

Bree

Everyone had stuff they were good at. Dot was good at knowing everything. Malia was good at being bossy. For a long time, Bree thought she was really only good at animal facts and making outfits and crafts involving glitter and knowing Taylor Swift facts and memorizing all the choreography from the musical *Cats*. But then they became spies, and everything changed. Bree found out what she was really good at.

After editing the clips from their mission to take down Seaside, she was the proudest she'd ever been. True, she had gotten a little bit of editing help from her stepdad, Marc, who had no idea what the video was for. But whatever. Bree was still proud of herself. And she seriously couldn't wait for her friends to be proud of her, too.

"Are you ready?" Bree asked as Dot and Malia sat, looking pretty ready. "I don't know if you're ready."

"Dude, we're ready. We've been ready for, like, five minutes," said Dot.

"Roll that beautiful footage," said Malia.

Bree pressed Play.

The first few seconds were exactly the same as the original Seaside Sitters testimonial video. "We love your children as much as you do," cooed Chelsea's voice as a sea of smiling child faces panned across the screen. "So trust them with the best."

Then there was a very dramatic cut. The screen went black and was underscored by scary heavy metal music. It was the same song Marc had used for one of his Go-Pro surfing videos. As the music played, footage of the Woo girls appeared, crying and screaming and stamping their feet. Next, one of the Larsson triplets came on-screen, picking his nose and then smearing it all over a very expensive piece of art.

"They taught my boys to speak Dutch!" said a gloating mom, from the original Seaside testimonial reel. Immediately afterward, the screen shifted to show footage of children sitting in front of a TV screen, playing a Rosetta Stone language learning tape, while Chelsea absentmindedly painted her nails.

"Speak Dutch!" she yelled, before turning her attention back to her nails. "I want to hear more pronunciation!" she screamed, while the children looked terrified.

"They cleaned my garage!" chirped another happy testimonial. Then time-lapse footage showed little Jackson, hauling bags of garbage out of the Woos' garage, moving a bunch of boxes that are almost as big as he is, sweeping the floor, and raking leaves. *Meet Jackson,* read the screen. *Only six years old. Hired by Seaside to clean this garage for the low price of one candy bar.*

The video neared its end with very dramatic instrumental music, the kind you'd hear during a movie when the dinosaur is about to eat everyone, or the hurricane is about to touch down. Bree borrowed it from the movie *Sharknado,* which was basically both of those things, but at the same time.

Your children deserve better, read the screen. Know the truth. *NO MORE SEASIDE.* Then everything faded to black.

Bree turned to her friends, satisfied.

"Wow," said Dot.

"That was . . . genius," Malia agreed.

"That deserves to win the highest award at, like, Cannes or something," Dot said. "Where did you learn how to do that?"

Bree just shrugged.

"I had no idea you were so good at editing," said Malia. "I'm seriously impressed."

Bree grinned. Forget the whole jelly bean counting contest, or even her birthdays the years she turned four, six, seven, nine, ten, and twelve, or even that time they sang "Ging Gang Goolie" at the choral performance; *this* was the new happiest moment of her life. The part where she had help creating the video would remain her little secret.

"Now we just have to figure out how to take this public without people knowing it's us," said Dot.

"Um, you guys? It's already public," Bree said.

"What do you mean?" Malia asked.

"Like, did you notice *where* the video is playing?"

Bree scrolled up so they could see what she meant. The video she'd played for them wasn't only live on the Internet, it was embedded on the Seaside Sitters' actual site. She'd painstakingly followed a tutorial she found online, which took her step-by-step through how to hack into the back end of Seaside's site and replace their gushing testimonial video with this special one, embedded right from YouTube.

"I pushed it live before you got here," Bree said.

"So the cat's already out of the bag," said Malia.

"Who put the cat in a bag?" Bree said. Now that she thought about it, she hadn't seen the cat in a while.

"It's just a saying," Dot said.

"Ooh! I know how to make it even better," said Malia with a devilish grin. Her expression looked like the time last year when she swapped out Chelsea's shampoo with conditioner so Chelsea would have greasy hair just in time for homecoming. "Maybe our good friend Ramona Abernathy would like to revive her account and send a few emails about it."

She pulled out her phone and began typing. Her fingers flew across the screen as she cleared her throat and started reading aloud in the snooty, high-pitched voice she had reserved for fake Abernathy emails:

"Dear Dina and Erika Larsson, I thought you might appreciate this video. Are these the same girls you hired for your epic family party? Perhaps you should reconsider. What a shame! Quality sittery is so hard to find."

"Sittery is still not a word," said Dot.

"Yes, I am aware of that. But it worked last time," Malia spat back. "What's that saying? Don't fix what's not broken."

"But wrong is kind of the same as broken," Dot replied.

Malia finished typing the rest of the email, in silence this time, and sent it off into the world.

"Wow. You guys, it seems like there's already quite a response!" said Dot, excitedly tapping her phone. "Look how many views the video has gotten already!"

Every time she kept hitting refresh, the number of views kept changing. They watched the number climb higher and higher. Normally, anything Bree posted (videos of Taylor Swift the cat wearing Emma's doll's clothes) got ten views (where at least five of them were Bree), but this was unlike anything she had ever seen. It seemed like everyone in town was watching and then sharing it with everyone they knew.

And then Malia's phone rang. She held up the screen so Bree and Dot could see it. *Dina & Erika Larsson*. Had they seen the email?

"What are you waiting for?" Dot practically leaped across the room. "Answer it!"

Dot and Bree couldn't hear the other side of the conversation, but they really didn't have to.

"I know, it's so shocking," Malia kept saying. Then finally, "Of course we'd be happy to watch all thirty-three kids at your family reunion next week . . . " She paused while Mrs. Larsson kept talking. "Wonderful. Full rate, per child, sounds more than fair. See you next week!"

When she hung up the phone, they did a collective dance

of joy. Bree put on celebratory music (which may or may not have been the opening number from *Cats*), and the three of them hugged and jumped and screamed.

"You did it!" Malia yelled, dancing happy circles around Bree.

"*We* did it!" said Bree.

They had finally, finally succeeded! And they had done it together.

CHAPTER TWENTY-FOUR

MALIA

Once again, pizza night was paying its weekly visit to the Twiggs family. But tonight, Malia barely touched her topped-with-everything slice. She didn't have time to eat, because she was so busy doing something she typically never got to do on pizza night (or, really, any night): She was speaking. Uninterrupted. About herself.

Ever since the news broke about the Seaside Sitters, Chelsea had gotten grounded, and Malia had stepped into a very unfamiliar place: the spotlight.

"It's like, *Kristy's Great Idea* was right there, just waiting to be *my* idea," she said. Her parents nodded their heads vigorously. Chelsea rolled her eyes but didn't say anything. "And what's weird is, at the time, I didn't know that I was good at babysitting. I didn't know that I liked babysitting. Honestly, I had no idea that babysitting still existed outside of horror movies and apps for services that allow strangers to come watch your kids. But it turns out, I really love it!"

"It's so nice to see you excel at something," her mother said.

"And to see you so enthusiastic!" her dad added.

Chelsea made a sound like she was being strangled.

"Is something the matter, Chels?" asked their dad.

"Some pizza must have gotten caught in my throat," she said, with a small shrug.

Once her parents had turned their attention back to their plates, Chelsea narrowed her eyes at Malia.

Not one to be intimidated, Malia took this as a good opportunity to drive the point home further. "It is rare, however, for someone my age to start a successful business," said Malia. "There are plenty of teenagers who get part-time jobs or whatever, but how many twelve-year-old CEOs can you think of?"

"I really can't think of any!" said her dad with a chuckle.

"Starting the club has really inspired me to think of other interesting avenues to pursue. My goal is to have a highly diversified résumé by the time I start applying to colleges." Malia smiled sweetly in Chelsea's direction. She probably didn't think Malia knew words like "diversified." But she did.

The conversation came to a lull. Malia's dad smiled. Her mom took a sip of lemonade. Chelsea sulked.

At last, Chelsea spoke. "I'm full," she said. "May I be excused?"

"Your sister is still eating," said their mom.

Malia picked up her slice and took a bite. She chewed very, very slowly, smiling in Chelsea's direction.

"On second thought, I'm also not feeling well," Chelsea said.

"It's fine, I'm done anyway," Malia conceded.

Chelsea pulled her chair out from the table and quickly disappeared from the room.

Malia breathed deeply and made a mental note to enjoy this moment, and the sweet silence coming from Chelsea's now-vacant side of the table. It was something Malia wasn't used to hearing during family dinners: the sound of success.

Malia had a little ritual she liked to perform every night before bed. First, she liked to think of three things that had gone well that day. Usually, they were small things, like especially good cafeteria fries at lunchtime. (Since the Seaside takedown, though, coming up with three good things had been easier than usual.) Next, she liked to imagine what Connor Kelly was doing at that exact moment. (In truth, she liked to do this more often than just at bedtime.) Was he playing a video game? Was he brushing his teeth? Was he already asleep? Imagining the options, Malia climbed into bed and turned off the light.

She snuggled up next to Humphrey, her secret stuffed dog that she still cuddled with in order to fall asleep. None of her friends knew about Humphrey, and she wanted to keep it that way.

As she settled under the covers, Malia's door creaked open a couple inches. She squinted through the darkness to see Chelsea's face peering in, illuminated by light from the hallway.

"Brutus," Chelsea hissed, so low that Malia could barely hear it.

"Excuse me?" Malia asked.

"Gaston."

"Wait, what? Like the dude from *Beauty and the Beast*?"

"Cruella."

"Oh my god. Chelsea, seriously." Malia rolled her eyes.

"Scar."

"Congratulations on your expansive knowledge of traitorous characters."

"Peter Pettigrew!" Chelsea spat.

Finally, it was just too much. Both sisters started to giggle.

It wasn't exactly a cease-fire, but it was probably as close as they would come.

"Why is the upstairs hallway light still on?" their mom's voice rang up the stairs. "Both of you should be in bed by now."

And with that, Chelsea scurried away.

CHAPTER TWENTY-FIVE

Bree

Of course, we would be thrilled to babysit both of your children, and their turtle," Malia said into her phone, while giving Dot and Bree an enthusiastic thumbs-up.

The girls had called a very necessary meeting of the Best Babysitters Club, since business had exploded in the wake of their Seaside takedown. Malia's phone was ringing off the hook, and all sorts of jobs kept falling into their laps.

"That's officially the third gig we've booked today!" announced Malia as soon as she hung up.

Bree, perched in her usual spot atop Dot's bedspread, uncapped a marker and darkened in another unit on their (very sparkly) new earnings chart. Dot had insisted upon creating a revised, Taylor Swift–free poster to track their progress, but that hadn't stopped Bree from attacking it with glitter.

Little puffs of sparkles flew off the poster as Bree colored it in.

The updated chart had two columns: one for tracking money they'd actually made, and another for keeping track of their projected earnings. So far, the girls hadn't gotten paid since the job they stole from Chelsea, so their actual earnings column remained nearly empty. But their projected earnings column was (literally) off the chart. After the Larsson family reunion job, they would have enough money to secure the venue, and after the rest of their new bookings, they would have enough cash to throw the party of their dreams.

"We could have a chocolate fountain, maybe," Bree said. "Like the one at Sheila's party. Today at breakfast, Marc said he would help get us one. He might not have been listening, but still, he agreed." Bree had consistently been mentioning the party at their family breakfasts and had yet to hear her parents agree to anything specific. However, she had also never heard them say no, which she thought counted for a lot.

"We also have to decide which of the Marvelous Ray's add-on packages we want," Malia rattled on. "Option one is fake tattoos, which is kind of universally appealing. They also have an accessories package, with funny hats and pins and glow sticks and stuff. Or we could do a candy bar?"

"But if we already have a chocolate fountain, that's maybe a lot of sugar," said Bree. She didn't really know how much sugar was too much sugar, but her stepsister, Ariana, liked to say that *everything* had too much sugar. Bree could only imagine how Ariana would react to a chocolate fountain *and* a candy bar.

"No such thing as too much sugar," countered Dot. "This is a party, after all. But we do want variety. So let's make a mental note to load up on savory snacks, too."

"Connor Kelly loves mozzarella sticks," Malia announced. "After many days of observation, I've noted it's his most-ordered item from the school cafeteria."

"That is mildly disturbing," Dot replied. "Also, this isn't Connor's party."

"Well, I also love mozzarella sticks, and it is my party, so we should definitely have them," concluded Malia. Then she grew silent as she stared off into the distance. Her friends watched her, confused. Surely Malia couldn't be that mesmerized with Dot's vintage concert posters.

"Hello? Malia? Where are you?" Dot asked, clapping her hands.

"Oh! Sorry." Malia snapped back to attention. "I was briefly entertaining a fantasy in which Connor and I attempt to dunk our mozzarella sticks into the communal bowl of marinara sauce at the exact same time."

"Okay, and . . . ?" Bree trailed off, confused.

"We turn our gaze from the sauce bowl to see who else possesses the same level of enthusiasm about mozzarella sticks. Our eyes meet. Electricity." Once again, her face took on that faraway look.

"Wow," Dot said. "Okay, so besides fried cheese, what are our nonnegotiables?" Dot asked. "Like, what are the things we absolutely must have?"

"Thank you for the vocabulary lesson. For your information, I already knew what a nonnegotiable was," teased Malia.

"They say you teach what you most need to learn," said Dot, with a shrug. She wasn't sure what it meant, entirely, but it was something her mom's yoga friends liked to say, and it seemed to apply here.

"We need a theme!" said Bree, who hadn't heard of a nonnegotiable until that moment.

"Not cats," Malia and Dot said in unison.

"Taylor Swift?" Bree tried.

"No," Dot said.

"I'm out of ideas, then." Bree shrugged.

"I like party planning as much as you guys, and I hate to be the voice of reason, but should we maybe use this time to go over our game plan for the job at the Larssons' this weekend?" Dot suggested.

"How about we work on the Kid-Kits? That's productive," said Malia.

She began taking all sorts of craft items and random odds and ends out of a trio of plastic shopping bags, and spread the items all over on the floor. The other girls joined her, sorting the various items into organized piles.

"Kid-Kits" were an idea they had borrowed (ah-hem, stolen) from the Baby-Sitters Club books. Kid-Kits were just little boxes filled with craft materials, like markers and stickers, along with playing cards and little toys they'd found for next to nothing at the local craft store. The girls planned to debut the kits at the Larsson family reunion, where they would hopefully help to occupy the massive amount of children. Given what they were getting paid for the Larsson job, having these extra materials on hand seemed like a very worthy investment.

"You know, things have really changed since the Baby-Sitters Club members came up with this whole Kid-Kit idea. Like, most of our babysitting charges are more than content to stare at some kind of electronic device," said Dot.

"So?" asked Bree.

"So the idea of wooing children with markers and glue seems remarkably optimistic," Dot concluded.

"But think about all the ways we had fun when we were that age," said Malia.

"Or even all the ways we have fun now," said Bree.

"I guess, but that's more about just being together," said Dot.

"Yeah, like, we could all be locked in a room without anything to do, and we'd still find a way to have fun," said Malia.

"I have to say, I'm so happy that everything worked out in our favor," said Dot. "We deserve this." Her friends nodded in agreement. "So how are we feeling about the Larsson job?"

"We are feeling so ready," Malia confirmed. "We've been through this, like, a million times."

"We know what we're doing!" Bree chimed. "And I already made the matching shirts." They had decided to wear matching T-shirts to the Larssons', sort of like camp counselors, to make them look more official. Of course, no one else had actually seen the shirts except for Bree. She was keeping them under wraps for as long as possible, since they were covered in glitter.

"I'm really excited, you guys!" Bree said as Malia's phone started ringing once again.

"There's so much to look forward to!" Bree continued. "The Larsson job, and then my birthday, and then the fall break, and then the party!" She clapped her hands, as was her way. She truly couldn't remember a time when she'd been more excited.

CHAPTER TWENTY-SIX

Dot

"**W**elcome! We're so glad to have you here!" Dina Larsson said, greeting Malia, Bree, and Dot in front of her enormous home with an even bigger smile. Her teeth were so white they were almost glowing.

"Let me give you girls a little tour," Dina offered, ushering them in through the enormous wooden doors. Dot thought it curious that she decided to call it a "little" tour, as surely nothing relating to the Larsson home could ever be described as little. The outside was even huger than she remembered, while the inside was huger than she imagined.

"This is the foyer," she said, motioning to the cavernous space just inside the front doors.

A sweeping black marble staircase stretched between the home's three floors, while the ceiling soared upward forever. It went so high Dot swore there could have been an astronaut orbiting near wherever the ceiling actually began. In the center of the foyer, there was a giant golden sculpture of a pointy-nosed fish thing that glinted in the sunlight.

"Ah, yes, the narwhal sculpture was created by the artist Dar Yak Gingerpigeon, and is crafted entirely of twenty-four-karat gold," Dina explained.

"Wow," they all breathed. Dot wasn't sure what the particular symbolism behind this piece was, but she understood Dina's point: the thing was called a narwhal, and it was very expensive.

Next, Dina marched them quickly through the rest of the first floor, until they arrived at the massive sliding glass doors that led to the backyard.

"So that brings us to the yard," she said, gesturing to the sprawling lawn that better resembled a national park. "Where you'll be spending your day. I'd love if you could encourage the children to stay outside as much as possible. As you can see, half of the kids are already here."

Half? Staring out at the sea of children, Dot thought: this must be how Braveheart felt before he went into battle. Or Joan of Arc. Or one of those guys from *Star Wars*. She looked at her friend's faces as they took in the scene. They looked excited, exhilarated, and ready.

"Hello, Aunt Dina!" said a cute little girl in a black-and-white-checkered dress, waving politely from the lawn. "I am so excited to be here today." The little girl beamed.

"Thank you, Samantha."

Well, at least the kids seemed well behaved.

"I'm sure you girls will be just fine," Dina said, flashing her glowing teeth. "But if you need me, I'll be over on the deck with the rest of the adults. Just flag me down if you have any questions." She disappeared into the house, leaving them alone with their charges.

"Hi, everyone!" said Malia, making her way closer to the swarm of children. "My name is Malia, and these are my friends Bree and Dot." Bree and Dot waved, somewhat awkwardly. "We're going to be in charge of you guys today, and hopefully we'll have a lot of fun together."

"Nice shirts," said little Samantha. Malia couldn't tell if her tone was sarcastic or sincere, but she was willing to give the kid the benefit of the doubt.

"Thank you! I made them myself," said Bree.

The matching T-shirts were something to behold. For

starters, they were rainbow tie-dye. On the back, each shirt had a huge *BB* printed on it, for Best Babysitters. The letters were, unsurprisingly, covered in rainbow glitter.

"We also made these boxes for you guys," said Dot, unpacking the giant tote containing the Kid-Kits. A couple children nervously approached. "There's stuff to make crafts, and cards, and games, and these neat little rubber dinosaurs including species from the Triassic, Jurassic, *and* Cretaceous periods!" Dot looked up. Both her friends and the babysitting charges were looking at her like she was insane. "Whatever, I think they're cool," she said.

A few of the children very slowly inched towards the Kid-Kits.

"It's okay," said Bree. "All this stuff is for you. You can do whatever you want with it."

A boy uncapped one of the markers and sniffed it.

"I'm going to play a game over there, okay?" said Samantha, pointing just a few feet away, to a very well landscaped Zen rock garden.

"Sure, that sounds fine," said Malia.

With that, Samantha took off, with five other kids trailing after her. The remaining few charges (including Bentley, the marker sniffer) sat down, gamely investigating the Kid-Kits.

"Have you guys ever made origami fortune-tellers?" Malia asked. Everyone shook their heads no. "What? Let me show you how. It's super easy and fun." Malia took it upon herself to demonstrate how to fold a piece of paper to create an origami fortune-teller, and then write numbers, words, and fortunes in each designated section.

Meanwhile, Dot lectured Bentley on various dinosaur groups. "This guy would be classified as Sauropodomorpha," she said, holding up a tiny toy dino, "because of his small head, long neck, and long tail." Bentley looked interested but also a bit confused. It was obvious he was only listening to Dot because he had a crush on her.

"Hey, guys, do we think it's okay for those kids to be riding their scooters so close to the edge of that cliff?" asked Bree. This is not a phrase one wants to hear ever, but especially not while babysitting.

"Wait, what?" Malia snapped to attention.

Sure enough, two little girls were zipping around on sparkly scooters, dangerously close to the bluff.

"SLOW DOWN!" shouted Malia as she raced over to corral the girls back to a safer spot.

Dot surveyed the yard. In the time it had taken the sitters to unpack their stuff and acquaint themselves with their surroundings, the other half of the party guests had arrived. Little kids were everywhere, dressed in everything from khakis to bow ties to baseball jerseys to frilly princess dresses. One small boy was inexplicably wearing a wet suit. There were skateboards and scooters and even a pogo stick.

Dot let out a deep breath. She felt like she might throw up a little. If she was being completely honest, she'd never seen so many children in one place. Little feet darted in every direction. So many tiny voices were talking at once that it was impossible to tell what any of them were saying.

She turned her attention back to the craft area, to spy Bentley coloring on another boy's face. Or rather, the boy's face was entirely covered in marker, and Bentley was slowly but surely making his way down the kid's neck.

"What are you doing?" Bree shrieked.

"Face tattoos," said Bentley, matter-of-factly.

"Okay, no more markers," Bree commanded, snatching the marker out of his hands.

"You said we could do whatever we wanted with this stuff!" he whined.

"Yes, because I thought you'd be reasonable!" she replied.

Over near the rock garden, formerly sweet Samantha

brandished an enormous stick like a sword. She was rounding up the troops to start some kind of revolution.

"Pirates!" Samantha shouted, encouraging a wave of cheers from the other children. "The time has come to rise up!"

Dot glanced down at her watch. They hadn't even been there for thirty minutes. How were they supposed to last all day?

By anyone's standards, this had turned into an intimidating crowd. Rowdy. Well rested. Already hopped up on sugar. Every age group was accounted for. Some of the older kids weren't any smaller than the sitters. Dot felt immediately outnumbered and incredibly lost.

"Don't eat that!" Malia yelled as a little boy picked a wild mushroom from the lawn and attempted to cram it into his mouth.

"HELP!" Bree yelled. Samantha and her band of "pirates" had bound Bree's wrists together and tied her to a tree. "Time for the big kid to walk the plank!" Samantha hollered as Dot and Malia raced to Bree's rescue.

"What are we going to do?" Dot asked as she did her best to untie Bree's wrist. Little kids and their tiny fingers were incredibly good at making knots. "This is horrifying. I'm actually afraid something terrible could happen."

"Where are the adults?" Bree moaned.

They looked across the lawn, over to the Larssons' deck, where the adults were having a nice, relaxed barbecue. They didn't seem to be aware of the bedlam unfolding mere meters away.

"Should we talk to Dina?" Dot asked. "She said to come to her with any questions."

"Absolutely not! We will not be defeated. We've got this. We just need a plan B." Malia snapped to attention. "All right. How about we divide the kids? There are thirty-three kids and three of us, so we divide them into teams of eleven. We can handle that. Right?"

"That still seems like kind of a lot . . ." Dot trailed off, skeptically.

"Do you have a better idea?" Malia snapped.

"Okay, how do we divide them?" Bree asked.

"Just grab eleven kids! Go!" Malia yelled.

And with that, they were off. Dot just hoped that didn't mean off the cliff.

Malia grabbed the group of pirate children, while Bree claimed the kids hanging out near the marker-free crafts area. That left Dot with the remaining eleven stragglers, including two boys on skateboards, three girls on scooters, and the kid wearing the wet suit.

"Let's split up into boys and girls!" yelled a boy in Bree's group. Six boys and five girls lined up on opposite sides of the yard, like they were about to play a game of Red Rover. The boy counted to ten. At the count of ten, the kids charged directly at each other, with no sign of stopping.

"What are they doing?" Dot asked a little girl.

"Oh, they're playing War. It's everyone's favorite game, but they outlawed it at school because everyone kept getting hurt."

Dot smacked her own forehead.

Sure enough, the boys and girls kept right on running until they'd collided into each other, landing on the ground in one big heap-o'-child. Luckily, no one seemed injured, but pretty much everyone cried.

Turning her attention back to the task at hand, Dot counted her charges (not an easy feat when they were zooming in every direction) and discovered there were only nine. Surely that couldn't be right. She counted again. Still nine. This was not good.

Where were the other two kids? Had they gotten mixed in with the pirate group? Had they . . . fallen off the cliff?

"Hey!" Dot yelled, rounding up the nine kids she was still

responsible for and sitting them down in a little circle. "We're going to play a game. It's called Frozen Children. You guys are going to sit right here and pretend to be frozen. You're going to stay absolutely still until I get back. If you don't move, you get a prize. If you do move, well, then a bear eats you. So don't move." The kids looked at her with very wide eyes as she took off running into the house.

As she made her way into the massive marble entryway, Dot heard giggling coming from somewhere above.

"Ready?" a little voice said.

Dot looked up to see Thor, one of the Larsson triplets, and his cousin Harry, flopped belly-down on top of their skateboards, almost like they were on a boogie board. They were about to attempt to skateboard down the steps, as if it were a water slide.

"What do you think you're doing?" Dot called. "Get off those skateboards and walk down the stairs." The boys begrudgingly did as they were told. "What is wrong with you? You could have gotten yourselves killed!"

"YOU'RE NO FUN!" yelled Harry, crossing his arms defiantly across his small chest.

"You know what's more important than being fun?" Dot asked. "Being alive." She grabbed them both by the shoulders and pointed them in the direction of the yard. "Now back outside where you belong, or I'm going to tell your parents you came in here without permission." The boys trudged slowly in the direction of the yard, with Dot close behind them. She was just exiting the Larssons' foyer, contraband skateboards in hand, when Malia sprinted up to the door. Malia stood, panting, looking like she might pass out.

"Have you seen a small child, about yea high?" she asked, holding her hand at waist height. "He may or may not be covered in mud?"

"Nope, haven't seen one," Dot said. As stressful as it was to feel like she was losing the battle of the children, she was oddly comforted by the fact that her friends were also struggling. Misery really did love company, she supposed.

"Can I have my skateboard back?" called Thor.

"Not a chance!" she said. Thor shrugged and continued on his way outside the house.

Suddenly, Malia and Dot heard a muffled crying sound. They glanced around, expecting to see a child having a breakdown, but instead they saw Bree, crouched under a decorative side table, her head in her hands. Lord knew where her eleven charges were or what trouble they were getting into. Dot reasoned it might be time to accept defeat.

"Bree? Are you okay?" Malia asked. Bree slowly climbed to her feet and made her way over to them.

"Should we call in some backup?" Dot asked.

"Backup? What does that mean?" asked Malia.

"I don't know, like, we talk to Dina about getting some of the parents involved. Or maybe your sister could come help out?" Dot suggested.

"We could use another person. Plus, Chelsea is pretty scary," Bree agreed.

"Over my dead body!" Malia yelled.

"Then how about asking one of the adults from the party? Just to maybe, like, yell at them a little?" ventured Bree.

"How could you even suggest such a thing? What kind of friends are you?" Malia screamed.

"We're trying to do what's best for everyone," Dot said.

"We? What is this? It's like you guys are ganging up on me!" Malia shrieked. Her voice had gotten really high and screechy, like a murderous hyena.

"No one's ganging up on anyone. We're all really trying our best," Dot said slowly.

"This isn't personal," Bree added. "We just got in a little over our heads."

"I don't know what's gotten into you guys, but we are not

ready to admit defeat. Failure is not an option! We don't have a choice!" Malia angrily waved her arms.

"I think you need to consider the bigger picture here," Dot said. "It might be time to swallow our pride."

"Speak for yourself!" Malia spat at Dot.

"This isn't a contest, Malia."

"Alia!" she yelled. For goodness' sake. Dot thought she had given up on that. "And everything is a contest! Everything is a contest and I always lose!"

"We aren't even doing that bad of a job!" Bree said. "It's just so many kids."

"We don't want anyone to get hurt. Please, let's just ask for help, before something crazy happens."

No sooner were the words out of her mouth than a terrible crash rang out through the house. The girls turned and scurried in the direction of the commotion.

The little boy in the wet suit stood in the foyer, next to the golden statue. He wailed as tears rolled down his face, though by all accounts he didn't appear to be injured. Next to him, a bicycle lay on its side, its front wheel still spinning. How on earth did he get that in here? Had they been so distracted that a kid had managed to *bicycle* into the house?

"It . . . it was an accident," he said, in a small voice.

"Oh my god," gasped Malia.

The girls' eyes widened as they surveyed the damage. The downed bike was the least of their worries—the golden tusk had come loose from the rest of the sculpture and was now making its way across the foyer. The girls watched as it rolled along, making a sickening metallic sound.

"The fish thing broke," breathed Bree.

"It's a narwhal," said Dot, then added, "the unicorn of the sea."

"What's going to happen?" whispered Malia, once again looking like she might pass out, but for real this time.

Erika Larsson appeared in the doorway, her hands on her hips. From the look on her face, they already knew the answer. The world, as they knew it, was over.

CHAPTER TWENTY-SEVEN

MALIA

"What am I going to tell my parents?" Malia searched her friends' faces for answers, but they looked as bewildered as she felt. She thought she would definitely puke.

"What are any of us going to tell our parents?" whined Bree.

"We'll tell them the truth," said Dot. "That we bit off way more than we could chew and got fired from a giant babysitting job. That a kid we were supposed to be watching crashed his bike into a priceless piece of art, and now we may or may not be responsible for paying for it, for what will probably amount to the rest of our lives."

"This is the saddest I have ever been," said Bree, stopping to sit down on the curb.

The girls were banished from the Larssons' house

immediately after the incident. Malia had never seen anyone look more furious than Erika Larsson had when she discovered the broken sculpture. With no other plan in place, the girls walked slowly in the direction of Poplar Place, shocked expressions on all of their faces.

"But . . . But . . ." Malia looked around in disbelief. "I don't think you understand. My parents were finally proud of me for, like, the first time in my life. Now I'm going to go right back to being 'Malia, the one who screws everything up.'"

Dot sighed. "Malia, I know what went down today totally sucks, and I'm really not looking forward to telling my mom about it, either," Dot spoke in an overly Zen voice that Malia found more frustrating than calming. "But it was also an accident. It doesn't make you a bad person. It doesn't even make you a bad babysitter. It just makes you a human businessperson who messes up sometimes and who is learning from her mistakes."

"Oh, please!" snapped Malia, with so much force that Dot actually took a step backward. "That doesn't make me feel better! It's so easy for you to talk down to me from your high mountain where you know everything. But you don't know what it's like to be me!"

"That is so unfair—" Dot started.

"You guys, please don't fight," said Bree, still sitting on the curb.

"It's just like when we were at the house"—Malia gestured behind her, in the general direction of the Larssons' house—"I wanted to soldier on! But you wanted to give up. You didn't have my back!" Her friends just looked uncomfortable. "This club is everything to me. And this job was our one big chance to prove ourselves. But look what happened! It was a complete disaster!"

"Yes, it was. But what's done is done." Dot sighed.

"What's wrong with you? It's like you don't even care!" Malia spat back.

"Of course I care. But you know what, Malia? Being good at babysitting isn't a magical answer to all your problems. It isn't going to make you as good as your sister!" Dot's voice got higher and higher as she continued. "It isn't going to make Connor notice you! It's not going to change anything at all!"

Malia gasped. She couldn't believe what she was hearing. This was her best friend, of all people. How could Dot be so mean?

"Stop fighting! Stop fighting! Stop fighting!" yelled Bree, covering her ears with her hands.

"And you know what?" Dot prattled on. "Even if we earned

the money to have this party, it's just a party. The very next day, you would still wake up as Malia, a person with a chip on her shoulder. A person who lives in her sister's shadow because she can't step up to claim the things she actually does well." Dot crossed her arms, apparently satisfied with herself.

"Are you kidding me right now?" Malia yelled. "I thought we were in this together." She had never felt more betrayed.

"You guys, can you please not fight?" wailed Bree, standing up so she was on the same level as her friends.

"Just SHUT UP, Bree!" Malia snarled. "Nothing you say ever makes anything better!" She felt bad as soon as she'd said it, but the words were already out.

Bree gasped.

"You're both mean!" Bree shouted. "You're both horrible! The two of you think you're so much smarter than me. But you know what? You're not. I'm the only one who's always nice. And that is so much more important!"

"WHAT ARE YOU SAYING, BREE? Are you saying I'm not nice?" Dot spat.

"Yeah, Bree, what are you getting at?" said Malia.

Bree opened her mouth to respond, but before she could make a sound, Malia exploded with rage. "You know what? Forget you guys. I don't need you. I can babysit all on my own!"

Malia was so angry at this point that she was practically vibrating. "THIS WAS MY BIG CHANCE TO PROVE MYSELF AND NOW EVERYTHING IS RUINED!"

"Malia," Dot spoke slowly, using that annoying therapist voice, "nothing is ruined."

"Yes it is! IF YOU WERE MY REAL FRIENDS, YOU WOULD UNDERSTAND!" Stupid tears were running down her face, and snot was right behind it. "I'LL BE BETTER OFF WITHOUT YOU." With that, she took off running.

Malia sprinted down the street, in the direction of Poplar Place, never turning back to look at her friends. She didn't know if they were following behind her, but she didn't care. They weren't behind her in life, the way that real friends should be, and that was all that mattered.

CHAPTER TWENTY-EIGHT

Bree

B **ree's** thirteenth birthday fell just two days after the Larssons' party, during the school's fall break. So far, it was the saddest birthday ever—even worse than the time Marc hired that really terrifying party clown because he hadn't married her mom yet and was trying to impress everyone, but the clown was so scary it made Bree hide under the deck and cry for, like, three hours. She didn't think a birthday could be worse than that one. But this year, it was.

Bree checked her phone every two minutes, waiting for her friends to wish her a happy birthday. For most of the afternoon, she didn't even bother to put her phone down, because she kept looking at it so often. But no one texted. No one called. Well technically, Shoko and Mo both did. But that's not who she was waiting for.

Dot, Malia, and Bree hadn't spoken since the incident at the Larsson house. All of their parents had spoken a whole lot, since they had to come up with some sort of plan to cover the cost of the narwhal sculpture. Luckily, after much discussion, Dina Larsson didn't expect them to pay for it.

Still, none of them reached out.

Losing the babysitters club was the worst thing that had ever happened to Bree. It was even scarier than the time she forgot all the words in chorus, because that time, her friends were there to back her up. Now she had no one.

The truth was, she had never cared about the money, and she hadn't even cared that much about the party. Sure, parties were fun and all, but the important thing was celebrating her friends. They had always found a way to celebrate each other, and not even elephant rides or chocolate fountains or whatever was going to change that. (A Taylor Swift performance could maybe change things, though. That could change anything.) Without Dot and Malia, the world was like a pair of sparkly shoes after all the glitter had fallen off. (In case this has never happened to you, it's really, really sad. And you can't glue it back on.)

Had they actually forgotten Bree's birthday? Did they just not care? Were they ignoring her on purpose? She didn't know which of those was the worst. She didn't know where to go from here.

"Happy birthday to me . . . Happy birthday to me . . ." she sang softly.

Bree was so sad that it inspired Taylor Swift the cat to come into her room and sit on her lap. She never did that, but she must have sensed Bree's sadness with her psychic animal nature. Normally, Bree had to bribe the cat to hang out with her, using food and toys. Bree should have been happy, but she didn't even care. This was a pity hangout, and it kind of hurt her feelings.

"Bree, love! What are you doing? Do you want to get ice cream?" her mom called from downstairs.

Even ice cream sounded sad to her. She didn't have much of an appetite. But she guessed it would be nice to go outside.

"Okay," she called back.

"Everyone! Let's meet out in the car!" Marc hollered.

Bree slowly climbed to her feet, stopping in the bathroom to check out her appearance. Her hair was shooting all over the place, and her eyes looked red and puffy from crying. Sigh. She brushed her hair and put on some of her sparkly rose-gold lip gloss. At least that was one good thing about today. Lip gloss is always a good thing.

Then she went downstairs and headed to the garage. It

was empty. Bree walked out into the driveway, but it was also empty. Where was everyone?

She ran down the front walkway and into the street, to see the rear lights of Marc's minivan way down the road. Everyone was already on the way to get ice cream. Her family had left without her. They were off celebrating the birthday of the person they forgot.

Bree went back inside.

"Meow," said Taylor Swift.

"Taylor Swift, will you hug me?" she asked.

The cat offered her a sad glance, then walked away.

CHAPTER TWENTY-NINE

MALIA

Everything in Malia's world was so depressing. School, which had never been anything but meh, certainly wasn't getting better. Connor Kelly had shown no further signs of being aware of her existence. And then there was Chelsea, the human equivalent of Styrofoam. No matter how much you tried to get rid of her, she wouldn't sink, she wouldn't crumble, and she would never, ever go away.

"Who needs some babysitting club when you can have an internship with Ramona Abernathy?" she said, breezing right by Malia on her way to her new, impressive job. Apparently, Ramona was no stranger to the tactics of jealous competitors, and the Seaside takedown had only served to endear Chelsea to her even more. And Chelsea was more insufferable than ever. She had actually started carrying a briefcase. Still, Malia didn't even feel the urge to trip her. She guessed this is what they called surrender.

As for her friends, Malia had never felt more betrayed. If she stopped to think about them for even a moment, she felt so angry and sad that she had to immediately think of something happy, like the way Connor Kelly's bangs flopped ever-so-perfectly over his left eye in his yearbook photo.

To make matters worse, it was Bree's birthday and Malia didn't know what to do. She picked up her phone approximately one million times. She should say something, shouldn't she? But that felt like giving in. What if Bree didn't respond? Or was hanging out with someone else? Or . . . Malia didn't know. Nothing felt right.

She decided to go for a walk around the neighborhood, "to rejuvenate the senses," as her mother would say. But everything she encountered made her feel even worse. She walked past the houses of all the families they'd tried to babysit for. She walked past the smelly old library, where she'd found that copy of *Kristy's Great Idea*. She walked all the way to the school sports field, where a pack of boys were loitering near the bleachers. She guessed she should have turned around before anyone saw her wandering around by herself like some kind of weirdo. But then one of them waved at her, and Malia knew it was too late.

She would recognize that wave anywhere. It was Connor Kelly. He galloped over to Malia like some sort of antelope, but, like, a really attractive one.

"Oh, hey, Malia," Connor said. He acted kind of surprised to see her, except he had just walked toward her on purpose, so of course that couldn't be true.

Malia stood there, stunned, like a tiny mammal in one of those nature videos when it sees a hawk approaching. This wasn't fair! Why did Connor decide to talk to her when she wasn't in her right mind? She'd been moping for days — she couldn't be expected to make words. Without a doubt, this was one of the most important moments in her social life thus far and she wasn't even prepared to deal with it.

"Too bad your party never happened," Connor continued with a shrug. "But Violet Van Gooch is having that huge party on Friday. So I guess everything turned out okay."

"Hmm?" Malia said. Violet Van Gooch was an eighth-grader. A very popular eighth-grader. And this was the first she had heard of the party.

"Were you invited?" he asked.

"Umm . . . I don't seem to have gotten my invite yet," Malia said.

SAY THAT I SHOULD GO ANYWAY, Malia silently

willed him. *SAY I CAN BE YOUR DATE, AND YOU WILL COMPLIMENT MY SHIRT AND SHARE A MOZ-ZARELLA STICK WITH ME.*

But instead he said, "Hmm. Okay." And just like that, he turned and sauntered off with his pack of boys. Huh? It was like the hawk in this nature video didn't even want to eat the tiny mammal. It was barely important enough to register.

Malia stood there, stunned. She most certainly was not invited to Violet's huge and impressive party. And now Connor Kelly knew that for sure.

Under normal circumstances, this was her worst nightmare coming true. On a normal day, she would have cried. Then she would have done everything in her power to snag an invite to that party. But today, it didn't matter. Nothing mattered. Malia felt like she had nothing left.

CHAPTER THIRTY
Dot

Normally, Dot lived for long weekends, because she was a human person and that was the socially acceptable thing to do. But the fall break weekend seemed to drag on into eternity. Nothing had ever felt like less of a holiday.

"How is it only Monday?" Dot wondered aloud.

Dot had already read everything in her exhaustive "to-read" pile. She had eaten so many contraband Oreos she was starting to get sick of them. She had even participated in her mother's prenatal yoga class with a dozen pregnant women, in the hopes it would impart some much-needed Zen. But still, she felt bothered.

This was why one should never go into business with friends, Dot thought. You wind up losing both your friends and your business. And then you've lost everything. Or more accurately, everything but sugar.

Things had gotten so bad that Dot had even started wearing the compass around her neck, in the hopes it would help her to tap into her internal compass. But without her friends, she felt lost. It suddenly didn't matter which direction she went, because when she got there, she would still be alone.

"Dot?" Her mom stuck her head in the door just as Dot was shoving the package of remaining Double Stuf Oreos underneath a stack of notebooks in her desk drawer.

Her mom paused in the doorway, nose in the air, like a police dog sniffing for drugs.

"Did I hear a wrapper?" she asked.

"No," Dot lied.

"Okay." She seemed satisfied, for now. "Is something the matter? I can't help but notice you've been sulking around all weekend."

"I'm almost a teenager. Pubescent hormones and sulking go hand in hand, do they not?"

Dot really wasn't in the mood to talk about it.

"Perhaps, but this seems even more pronounced than usual," her mom said. Dot felt grateful to have such a perceptive mother. Sometimes it was annoying when Dot would have preferred to fly under the radar, but in moments like this one she welcomed it. She immediately ruined it by adding, "Plus, I'm sure whatever is going on isn't aided by the fact that Mercury is currently in retrograde."

"Okay, so Malia and Bree and I got into a giant fight, over what happened at the Larssons'."

"Oh, I know. Are you forgetting the hundreds of phone calls about narwhals and metalsmiths that I had to endure?" She rolled her eyes. Instead of being mad at Dot for what happened, her mom's reaction had been one of disgust for the amount of materialism that was apparently running rampant in Playa del Mar.

"I think Malia had been looking at this whole babysitters thing as a chance for her to prove once and for all that she's as impressive and responsible as her sister. And everyone was so excited about this party, and we lost sight of what really mattered."

"Look, Dot. Relationships are complicated," her mom said.

"Yeah, but we all said some pretty nasty things about each other. I'm afraid that even if we were to start speaking again, we aren't going to be able to take them back."

"Any time you put different people together, there is bound

to be conflict. Different thoughts and feelings, different opinions, different hopes and dreams . . . sometimes, having arguments is inevitable. It's what you do next that really counts."

Dot thought about that for a moment. She knew her mom was right. But what if, during the course of the argument your feelings got hurt? Or you discovered a side of your friend you didn't like very much?

"You girls have been friends for a long time," her mom continued. "I'm sure that both of them are having just as hard a time as you are this weekend."

"Somehow I doubt that," Dot said. She pictured Malia having a grand old time at Marvelous Ray's, or spying on Chelsea, or chasing Connor Kelly around town with her phone camera and trying to secretly film him eating a mozzarella stick.

"You don't have any plans to see one another? Not even for Bree's birthday?"

Dot shook her head. "We're technically supposed to have a babysitting job tomorrow. This little boy named Aloysius is coming back from mini Mensa camp and the three of us are supposed to watch him after school."

"Have any of you been in touch to confirm?" her mom asked.

"No. I'm planning to show up, because I really like him,

and I don't want to let his mom down. But I have no idea if the others will go. We're technically not a club anymore, so . . ." Dot trailed off. "It's just . . . I'm afraid. I'm afraid that even if we see one another, even if we apologize, no one is going to be able to forget what everyone else said about them. What if we can't get past that?"

"You know, Dot, people think that forgiveness is a thing you do for other people. But forgiving your friends isn't just something you do to make them happy. Forgiveness is also a gift for yourself."

"What do you mean?"

"It's not good to hold on to hurt feelings, or to spend a lot of time thinking about things that make us upset."

That was for sure. Dot was driving herself crazy replaying the narwhal incident over and over, but it was only making things worse.

"See what your friends have to say," her mom continued, "and do whatever feels right to you. But remember, no matter what happens with the club, or even with your friendships, you can always choose to forgive them."

"Thanks, Mom," she said. Dot had to admit that she had a point.

"I'm so happy to see that you're wearing your compass!"

her mom said, leaning in for a hug. If only the compass could point the way toward forgiveness, Dot thought. Or better yet, if only the compass could somehow lead her back to the past, when everything had been perfect, but she didn't know to appreciate it.

CHAPTER THIRTY-ONE

MALIA

When Malia arrived at Aloysius's house, both Bree and Dot were already there. Malia felt nervous but not surprised. It was just like both of them to do the goody-two-shoes thing and show up where they were expected.

The truth was, Malia almost didn't go. She had stayed up thinking the night before, trying to figure out whether or not she was ready to see her friends. She was done being angry. Now she just felt embarrassed about what went down at the Larssons, and in a larger sense, with the entire club. She had wanted them to form the club for three reasons. The first was obviously to raise money for an epic party, to cement her place in Playa del Mar history as somebody who mattered. The second reason was to build something together, with her two best friends. The third reason was harder to admit. In her heart, Malia had wanted to start a babysitting club because she thought that maybe it was finally something she could be good at. (She wasn't sure exactly why she thought this, since she never even particularly liked small children, but whatever.)

All around her, everyone else seemed to have their "thing." Dot was good at science. Bree was good at singing and dancing. Chelsea was good at everything. Malia thought taking charge—of a club, of little kids, of the plans for a party— could be her thing. When everything imploded, she felt like a total failure, and now even her friends thought she was a loser. As much as she missed them, she wasn't ready to see them.

But now, as if by magic, the three of them were together again. Well, *together* might be a strong word, since they hadn't actually acknowledged one another. But all three of them were in Aloysius's room, so that was something. For an awkwardly long while, nobody spoke. The three of them stared at their phones, absentmindedly tapping away while Aloysius sat on his bed, reading the dictionary. Finally, he closed the giant book with a thud.

"Okay. *I'm* supposed to be the one who doesn't talk here. What's going on?"

He crossed his tiny arms. Bree, Dot, and Malia glared at each other, but no one spoke. Aloysius looked back and forth, intently examining each of them.

"I wasn't gone for *that* long, and now you're not speaking to one another?"

None of them said anything. Bree just shrugged.

"All right, fine. You've left me no choice but to weigh in on your body language," he said with a sigh.

He pointed to Malia. "She's angry because she doesn't feel appreciated. She feels like she put a lot of effort into something, and she's disappointed it didn't work out."

Next, he pointed to Bree. "She's just sad. Really, really sad."

Finally, he pointed to Dot. "She just wants everyone to make up and be friends again, largely because fighting is very inefficient and she wants to move on with life."

Then he stepped in the middle of the room. "But you— all three of you—have a lot of love for one another. That is clear to see. I saw it that day at the cat café, and I saw it the last time you babysat. Believe me, good friends are valuable, and you can't just let that go. You can't let your frustration get in the way of how much you care. And you can't waste time being angry when you could be busy creating more wonderful memories together."

They all just sat there, dumbfounded. What was up with this little kid? Where did he learn this stuff?

"Now," he continued, like he was leading some kind of self-help seminar, "I'm going to go around the room and I want each of you to name one thing you love about the other two."

He pointed to Malia. "Malia, you go first."

Ugh. Well, that wasn't fair. Why did she have to go first? Malia thought for a while. Should she be honest? Of course there were lots of things she loved about both of her friends, but what if they didn't have anything nice to say about her? Finally, she spoke.

"Bree, you are so special. I loved when you ate that weird twig thing Dot's mom served us at her house that time. You probably think no one notices, but I know that you do things because you care and you don't want other people to feel bad or get hurt. You're probably the nicest person I know."

Bree gave Malia a little smile. "Yeah, that twig thing was weird," she confirmed.

"Dot, I love how you apparently know everything." Dot shot Malia a look like she might kill her. "No, no, don't take that the wrong way! I'm not suggesting you're a know-it-all. I'm saying you literally know everything. I love how you're wise. You understand feelings and thoughts and you have such great

231

insight into every situation. Sometimes I wish I could be more like you."

"Very good!" said Aloysius. "Dot, now it's your turn."

Dot took a deep breath. "Malia. I love that you're an idealist. I love how you believe in the power of dreams and you're not afraid to prevail, even when something seems out of reach or isn't the most logical. I love how you never give up. And, Bree, I love how you're full of surprises. Whether you're secretly learning how to code or breaking out into a spontaneous dance, being around you is always an adventure. I find that really inspiring."

"Can't . . . can't . . . speeeeeeeeeeeeak," said Bree in between sobs. "I love everything! I love all the things about both of you." Then she just cried and cried, which was essentially the same as her sharing specific things she loved about them.

"I really missed you guys," Malia said. "I love you both, and nothing is going to change that."

"I love you, too," said Dot.

"I'm sorry we missed your birthday," said Malia. "I thought about you the whole day."

"Yeah, happy birthday, Bree," said Dot. "We'll make it up to you."

Bree just sniffled.

Malia had never felt more relieved. Without her friends, nothing else mattered. And with them, everything else—Chelsea, her family, absolutely all of it—magically seemed okay.

Then, like they were characters at the end of a movie, they gathered in the center of the room for a group hug. They stood like that for a whole minute—the three of them embracing one another—until they felt a fourth set of arms come to encircle the group. Aloysius.

"You guys are my favorite people," Malia said. "I can't imagine doing this with anyone else."

"Little kids are still gross, though," said Dot.

"Hey!" said Aloysius.

"Not you," they both said with a laugh.

So maybe the girls weren't so bad at this, after all. And maybe, as they learned stuff, they could get better. Malia definitely wasn't ready to give up on the babysitters club, and she could tell her friends weren't, either. After all, what's that saying? Nothing that's good is easy? Yes, her friends, her evil sister, the realities of running a business—basically everything about the past few weeks—had been pretty annoying, and she still didn't have the answers. Even so, she couldn't help but admit that, together, what they had was really, really good.

CHAPTER THIRTY-TWO

Bree

Bree loved parties. What was not to love? The music, the dancing, the games, the food, the dedicated hashtags. So far this year, they had experienced epic parties— parties with elephant rides and confetti machines and performances by famous people. There were parties at bowling alleys and skating rinks and laser tag parks and swimming pools and mini golf courses. There were parties with food and parties with ice cream and parties that required getting all dressed up.

Then there were *their* parties—their bootleg backyard birthday celebrations. Bree looked forward to them every year. They may have been small by comparison, but those were always the very best parties, because they were theirs.

In the end, Bree, Dot, and Malia couldn't afford to throw a

magical bash at Marvelous Ray's. But after a few weeks of regular babysitting gigs, they had saved up *just* enough to throw a slightly tricked-out version of their usual backyard bash and convinced their families to help out. Marc went ahead and got them that chocolate fountain. Bree's mom got them a cake with a picture of the three of them on it. *Happy Birthday, Babysitters!* it read, in loopy red icing letters.

"That's kind of weird. I mean, I don't want anyone to eat my face," Dot said when she saw it. But Bree could still tell that she liked it.

"Let's get this show on the road!" said Malia, bursting into Bree's backyard in the most festive outfit she had ever seen Malia wear. Usually Malia was a jeans-and-sneakers girl, but today she wore a knee-length floral print dress with low platform sandals. She even had a flower in her hair. It looked like the kind of outfit Ariana would wear.

"Wow! Look at you!" said Dot, who was wearing a slightly fancier version of her usual black jeans-and-shirt combo.

"Connor Kelly said he was coming," Malia stage-whispered, glancing around suspiciously, even though none of the guests had arrived yet and there was no one to possibly overhear her.

For the next half hour, the three of them excitedly poured

snacks into bowls, tied balloons to chairs, and rearranged yard furniture so there would be more room for dancing. It felt a little like the prep before a Best Babysitters meeting but way more festive. Finally, they helped arrange the food Bree's mom had gotten catered from a local Italian restaurant—pizza, garlic knots, and, of course, mozzarella sticks.

"Where should Taylor go?" Bree asked, dragging her life-size cardboard cutout of Taylor Swift into the backyard. Her mom and Marc had given it to her for her birthday, as a way of convincing her to stop calling the cat Taylor Swift.

"Oh no. Over my dead body," said Dot.

"I thought we agreed. No themes," said Malia.

"Okay, fiiiiine." Bree sighed, walking cardboard Taylor back into the house. But before she reached the screen door, she stopped. "You know what?" she said, walking defiantly back toward the table, cardboard Taylor bopping along beside her. "I'm not giving in this time. This is my party, too, and this is my cardboard Taylor, and I want her to be at the party." Malia and Dot exchanged knowing glances. Malia shrugged.

"Can we not have her be so . . . front and center?" Dot asked.

"And not directly behind the food table," Malia added. "I know Connor Kelly will be spending a lot of time near the mozzarella sticks, and I don't want him to lose his appetite or anything."

Bree made an exasperated sound. "Brands hire Taylor as a spokesperson so they will buy their food. She's not going to cause anyone to lose their appetite. What kind of a CEO and marketing director are you guys if you don't understand that?" Bree dragged cardboard Taylor right next to the dance floor, which she reasoned was exactly where she belonged. "There!" she said, satisfied with herself.

As if on cue, music started pouring into the backyard. Dot had created a playlist, and Marc helped set up the speakers in tree branches so the music could pump into the yard at an even louder volume than usual.

"See? Our party has Drake, too!" Bree said, dancing a little bit to the first song on the playlist. "Who needs a black-tie bat mitzvah when you have this?"

"Of course, our Drake song is coming out of a stereo, while Charlotte Price's Drake song came straight out of Drake's mouth," said Dot. "But I do appreciate your enthusiasm."

The parents—Bree's mom and stepdad, Malia's mom and dad, and Dot's mom—filed out of Bree's house, where they had been talking about boring parent things like work and cars, and took their places around the yard to serve as helpers and chaperones. Dot's mom took her post beside the beverage table, giving the side eye to the vast assortment of soft drinks. Part of her personal contribution to the party was flavored sparkling water and also kombucha, which she would inevitably try to push on anyone looking for a drink.

Malia's parents, now joined by a begrudging Chelsea, loitered near the dance floor. Malia's dad did a little jig that, had anyone else witnessed it, would have easily embarrassed Malia for the rest of her middle school career. Luckily, her mom pointed to a vacant bench over near a flower bed, prompting the family to saunter over and take a seat.

At last, it was time for the guests to arrive. There was Shoko and Mo and Ivy and Stephanie and Charlotte and Sheila. There was Connor Kelly and his whole pack of surfer boys. Bree's stepsister, Ariana, even came with two of her friends, Alana and Amira. Bree sometimes wondered if they all became friends because their names sounded alike — so dramatic and pretty and adult.

"BIRT-DAY! BIRT-DAY! PUDDIN' PUDDIN'!" screeched Olivia as she toddled out of the back door and right up to the picnic table. Without wasting a moment, she reached her little arm out over the spread of food and then plunged it right into the special photo cake. She grabbed a fistful of icing in her little hand, then smeared it all over her face. Sure enough, the portion she had grabbed was right in the center of icing-Dot's face.

"Well, I guess the good news is, no one's going to eat your face," said Malia. "The bad news is, Olivia is now wearing it."

"CACK! CACK!" yelled Olivia. It sounded not unlike a cat choking on a hair ball, but it was her toddler way of saying "cake."

"Oh my goodness," Bree's mother said, scooping Olivia up into her arms. "I better take this one back inside and get her cleaned up."

"Woo-hoo!" yelled Mo. They turned to see Shoko demonstrating some fancy gymnastics moves near the patio. Bree scanned the yard, where everyone was laughing and having a good time. She was really proud of her friends.

Connor Kelly and the rest of the pack of surfers mostly stayed parked near the chip bar—which was sort of like a candy bar, but with every possible flavor (and texture!) of potato chip. (This was obviously Dot's idea.) The boys took turns taking handfuls from bowl after bowl, stopping periodically to clean the BBQ or cheddar or sour cream dust from their fingertips. Leave it to those boys to always resemble the grazing yaks from the nature channel, even in Bree's own backyard.

Malia, of course, kept her eyes transfixed on them no matter where in the yard she was.

"Go get some chips," Dot urged, elbowing Malia in the ribs.

"But I don't even like chips that much. And what would I say?"

"MALIA," Dot sighed. "It's not about the chips. You have been waiting for this moment for weeks. Do not forfeit this chance."

Malia slowly made her way over to the chip bar, stopping to look around the yard a couple times, like she was pretending to search for someone. It was a pretty good move. Then she stopped right in front of the table, scanning all the chip options. This was a pretty good move, too.

"Hey, Malia," Connor said.

"Oh! Yes, Connor?" Malia said, as though until that moment she hadn't noticed him standing there. She turned to face him, and they stood that way, mere inches from each other. It was so romantic and exciting. Dot and Bree held their breath.

"Chips are pretty good, huh?" Connor said, and turned his attention back to the rest of the surfers.

Malia scurried back over to Bree and Dot, looking weirdly excited.

After that, there was a lot of dancing—Bree may or may not have pulled out some of her moves from *Cats*, but with Katy Perry in the background, you could barely tell they were inspired by felines. Even Charlotte Price, who turned up her nose at everything, seemed to have a good time.

Bree's mom lit the candles—thirteen candles, and one for good luck—and everyone sang "Happy Birthday," which more than made up for her real birthday, when nobody did. The three girls blew the little flames out together, and Bree's birthday wish was that they could do this every year, forever.

"You want to hear something weird?" Dot asked, taking a bite of her cake. "I almost wanted to invite Aloysius."

"HA! I was thinking the same thing!" Malia said.

"Let's bring him a piece of cake when we babysit tomorrow," Bree suggested. Dot and Malia agreed.

As they continued eating their cake slices, Connor stopped right next to the table.

"Hey, Malia," he said.

She looked up at him, her fork halfway to her mouth.

"Yes?" she said, her voice quivering.

"These are good mozzarella sticks," he said, holding a spear of fried cheese in the air and nodding with approval. Then he walked away. Malia gazed after him with her mouth slightly ajar, the way one might after beholding a unicorn in the wild.

"Two interactions in one day!" Dot teased.

"That's all the birthday present that I need," Malia said with a sigh.

The rest of the afternoon flew by in a blur of eating and dancing and eating some more. And just like that, it was over.

"Cool party," said Connor Kelly, giving Malia a small wave before he and the surfers loped off into the distance. Bree still didn't understand why Malia found him so fascinating, but whatever.

After the party, the three of them gathered in the gazebo to gossip about everything that had happened, and of course, to look at what their classmates had posted on social media. It was so nice to be back in their usual spot. It was as though so much had changed, and yet, nothing had really changed at all.

"So, Malia and I chipped in on a little something for your birthday," Dot said, handing Bree a giant shopping bag filled with sparkly tissue paper. Bree reached her hand into the bag and riffled around until she felt something super soft and dreamy. She pulled it out of the bag and squealed with glee. It was the golden retriever from the toy store at the mall!

"Aw, YOU GUYS," Bree said, the tears already starting to well up in her eyes. "You shouldn't have. I mean, you should have. I mean, I'm so glad you did!" The dog's eyes were super glittery and his plush tongue stuck sideways out of his mouth. Bree loved him so much, both for his cuteness and also for what it meant. "Hi, doggy," she whispered, squeezing the retriever tightly so he would know he was loved.

"We waited until after the party to give it to you, because you know our feelings on interacting with stuffed animals in public," Dot said, doing her best to maintain an air of cool.

"I think this party was a success," said Malia.

"Definitely our best one yet!" Bree said.

"You know, seventh grade is actually shaping up to be much better than I thought," Malia said.

"Agreed. Even babysitting turned out to be pretty enjoyable." Dot laughed.

"I love you guys!" Bree said, because that was always the right thing to say.

"So," said Malia, her face lighting up in that familiar way. "I was thinking about the future of the club, and I have an idea. A really big idea."

"Uh-oh," groaned Dot. "This sounds awfully familiar."

"No, really, you're going to love it!" said Malia as the first fireflies of the evening started to blink all over Poplar Place. "I'm feeling . . . expansion."

"Expansion?" said Bree, her eyes growing wide.

"Yes. I think it's time for Best Babysitters to take our rightful place in this world as major game changers. Innovators. Thought leaders. Titans of the industry!"

"Okay, that just sounds like you're channeling Chelsea," said Dot.

"I'm kidding," said Malia. "Sort of. But I'm not kidding about the expansion part. I was thinking, maybe we can grow our organization. More members, more clients, more jobs, more money . . ."

"More fun?" said Bree.

"More buying power!" said Dot.

"More of everything," said Malia. "It's my best idea yet."

Bree wasn't entirely sure what it all meant, but it sounded great to her.

"Seriously, you guys, we are going places," said Malia, spreading her arms wide. No matter what happened, as long as they were together, all three of them knew that they would.

ACKNOWLEDGMENTS

My first thanks goes to Anne Heltzel—friend, colleague, co-conspirator (the list goes on)—without whom none of this would have happened.

Thank you to the wonderful humans at Alloy Entertainment, especially Lanie Davis, Josh Bank, and Sara Shandler. You are, quite possibly, the most fun group one could ever hope to share a conference room with.

Many thanks to the entire team at HMH for the magic of making this story into a book. An immense thank-you to Elizabeth Bewley for your enthusiasm and to Lily Kessinger for seamlessly taking up the reins.

I owe so much to Suzanne Gluck, Andy McNicol, and Eve Attermann, whose guidance and encouragement over the years has been a tremendous gift. Thank you for leading by example. I am beyond grateful to have you in my corner.

Ben Schrank, thank you for teaching me many things.

Brettne Bloom, thank you for demonstrating how encouraging words can change the course of a person's life. You have surely changed mine.

Thank you, parents, for giving me life and practically

everything that goes along with it. Mom, thanks for teaching me to read and for never saying no to a book, no matter how many I picked up. Dad, thanks for encouraging me to follow my passion, even though I actually took that advice. Poe and Uncky, thank you for being my best (and only) babysitters, which are some of my happiest memories. Thank you, Mia, for being underfoot during most of the writing process. I love you all more than words can express.

Ocean Township Library, thank you for children's story hour and for being my first employer. Thank you, Mark Fleming, for passing along the creative bug.

Love and thanks to my friends and early draft readers, especially Michael Freimuth, Alex de Lara, Rayhane Sanders, Jesse Aylen, Jessica Almon, Uli Beutter Cohen, Mike DeSutter, and Travis Brown.

Michael Mitnick, thank you for your encouragement. Full stop. Also, thank you for dinner.

Last but certainly not least, thank you to YOU, dear reader, for holding this book in your hands. I am so grateful.

BEING A BOSS ISN'T ALL IT'S CRACKED UP TO BE . . .

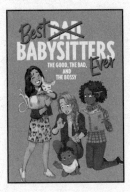

Just when Malia, Dot, and Bree (aka the Best Babysitters) corner the Playa del Mar babysitting market, their lives get even busier. Malia's evil older sister ropes her into a thankless internship. Dot *must* win the science fair. And Bree's brand-new cat turns out to be a holy terror. *Meow!* Malia is frustrated by the group's lack of commitment until she has an idea so great it rivals the creation of the club in the first place: they can hire new babysitters and take a cut of their wages! It's all of the money and less of the babysitting. This plan is too perfect to fail. Until—spoiler alert—it does, in the most hilarious way possible.

CHAPTER ONE

MALIA

Sometimes, if she tried really hard, Malia Twiggs could remember a time when she thought boogers were gross. It's not that she currently *liked* boogers — she hadn't gotten an entirely new personality or anything — but in the months since starting her own babysitting club, she had definitely learned to make peace with them. It was amazing, really, the limitless boundaries of personal growth.

"Don't worry about a thing!" Malia yelled, waving across the yard to her best friends and fellow babysitters, Bree Robinson and Dot Marino. "I've got this situation under control."

The situation at hand was a crying Jonah Gregory, their four-year-old babysitting charge who had just tripped while chasing a butterfly. The damage seemed to be two skinned knees and a lot of tears but, thankfully, nothing else.

Bree offered a little salute and Dot nodded before they turned their attention back to the other three Gregory children.

Malia calmly guided Jonah across the yard and into the house. As a now-experienced babysitter, she knew exactly how to clean and bandage his scraped knees, tell a goofy joke to put an end to the tears, and, yes, do away with his crying-induced snot.

"BUT IT HUWTS!" yelled Jonah, who could not yet pronounce the *r* sound.

"I know it hurts, but look how brave you are," Malia said, expertly applying a Band-Aid emblazoned with smiling cartoon rabbits. "And now that you're all patched up, I have a surprise for you."

Jonah continued to pout.

"You get to have ice cream!"

At the mention of a frozen treat, Jonah's small, chubby face visibly brightened.

Babysitting had taught Malia many things, including how easily little children could be bribed with snacks, how willing they were to believe whatever an older person told them, and, last but certainly not least, how nice it was to buy things with your own money. But on a deeper level, babysitting had shown her what it meant to transform. One day, you could be a regular seventh-grader with no crisis management skills whatsoever, and then, before you know it, there you were: herding four children around a home, all while making grilled cheeses, breaking up a fight, and negotiating nap time like it was nothing. For Malia (who, before the club, had always struggled with school and sports and every activity known to man), being good at something felt really, really nice.

Malia and Jonah made their way back to the yard.

"What? How come you get ice cream?" yelled eight-year-old Fawn, the oldest Gregory child, upon seeing Jonah's chocolate-dipped cone. She angrily crossed her arms.

"YEAH!" echoed Plum and Piper, the six-year-old Gregory twins. "Not fair!"

"Don't worry, I brought enough for everyone," said Malia, holding the box aloft.

"Not so fast. Everyone has to sit down before they can have some," said Bree with authority. As one of five siblings, Bree was an expert at dealing with little kids and generally navigating chaos. Immediately, everyone sat, and Dot distributed the cones.

Malia also remembered a time—around the same point when boogers were enough to trigger a meltdown—when a gig like this would have driven her and her friends over the edge. But now they could watch four children and actually enjoy doing it.

As the small ones devoured their ice cream, Malia craned her neck to peer over the chain-link fence, trying to catch a glimpse of the neighbors. The house next door was small and blue, with a gray-shingled roof and some spindly evergreen trees dotting the backyard. To most anyone, it looked like a regular old house. But to Malia, it was a place of endless wonder.

It wasn't the home itself that was magical, but the people who lived there, particularly one Connor Kelly (aka the only boy worth loving). That house was the place where he woke up each morning and played video games and ate waffles. Connor's jeans—the very same jeans he casually stuck his hands in the pockets of—were somewhere inside, along with his backpack and his T-shirts and his bike and his toothbrush. The toothbrush that touched his beautiful smile. Malia shivered. It was almost too much to handle.

"Any sightings?" asked Dot.

"Not yet," said Malia. But there was still hope.

For years, Malia had watched Connor float through the halls of Playa del Mar's public school system the same way her older sister watched the shoe sales at the local mall—with a laser focus. But now, thanks to the Gregory gig, the unthinkable had happened: Malia could observe him in his natural habitat. That is, if he ever came outside.

"MOM!" yelled the Gregory twins, at the sound of a car in the driveway.

Mrs. Gregory appeared at the gate, where a peaceful, controlled scene awaited her. This was the magic of babysitting. By this point, Jonah's accident seemed like a distant memory. Any traces of sugar had been discarded. This was a skill they had learned over time — the ways of the artful cleanup. In the early days, the parents might return home to find their children spinning wildly, like sugar-addled tops. But today, all Mrs. Gregory saw were the smiling faces of her four beloved children and the three somewhat older children who had kept them alive and relatively happy for the last few hours.

"I'll definitely be calling you again soon," said Mrs. Gregory as she counted out a stack of crisp bills. "My sister invited me to a luncheon next weekend, and we'll need someone to watch the kids."

"Of course!" Malia said.

"We'd love to," Bree added, nodding so vigorously that her dangling iridescent gemstone earrings twinkled in the light.

As the girls started down the driveway, Malia saw something

from the corner of her eye. It was orange. It was moving. OH MY GOD IT WAS HIM.

The orange blob was none other than Connor Kelly, sauntering down his front lawn. The only thing standing between them was the Gregorys' chain-link fence (and about a stratosphere's worth of middle school politics, but really, who was counting?). Malia couldn't breathe. Her excitement level was like she'd seen a pop star and a movie star and a YouTube star and an actual star from the sky, all at the same time.

"Hi!" Malia said, so softly she barely heard it herself. It reminded her of how sometimes, when she ordered at the school cafeteria, some boy would place his order at the exact same moment as she did, but speak way louder, and no one would hear her voice.

"Hi?" Malia squeaked, a little louder.

Connor didn't seem to notice.

"Hi!" Malia said, at a volume that was unfortunately loud. This time Connor looked up.

"Oh, hey," he said, brushing his floppy hair off his forehead.

A bird chirped. Malia swore the sun began to shine a little brighter. Or was she just about to pass out? HOW WAS HE REAL?

"Um, okay," Malia said.

"Okay what?" Connor said.

"You know, just saying hi. Hi!"

"Hi," said Connor.

In her frequent daydreams of this situation, Malia was bursting with topics to discuss with imaginary Connor. But now, faced with real Connor, she couldn't think of a single thing to say. She glanced awkwardly down at her sneakers. Luckily, Connor interrupted the silence.

"So, I just found out I'm going to a concert," he said.

"Right now?" Malia asked. Maybe she could go, too.

"No, in three weeks," he said. "Veronica's coming to the Arts Center."

Malia gasped. Veronica (simply "Veronica," no last name necessary) was the biggest superstar imaginable. In the past year, she and her blue hair had skyrocketed to fame unlike anything ever witnessed before. Even Bree had virtually abandoned her love for Taylor Swift when faced with the glory of Veronica.

"Oh! Yeah, me too," said Malia. The lie escaped before she could realize what was happening.

Truth be told, Malia had never really caught Veronica fever. She thought Veronica was just *okay,* with her endless rotating wardrobe and her larger-than-life concerts. But Malia vowed then and there that no matter what it took, she would be at that show. It was the event of a lifetime—not because of Veronica, but because of Connor.

"Yeah, Charlotte's dad got a box for the concert, and everyone is going," said Connor. "Aidan, Bobby, Violet, Mo . . ."

"And me!" said Malia, with perhaps a bit too much force. "So I'll definitely see you there."

"Yeah. Sounds great," said Connor, sweeping his floppy hair away from his perfectly sun-kissed forehead.

"I can't wait! I mean, to see Veronica. I mean, of course." Malia started walking backward, away from the fence. "Enjoy the rest of your day!" As she tried to scurry away before any more words could escape her mouth, she stumbled over a tiny shrub. She quickly popped back up and retreated in a manner that she hoped looked very calm but feared looked rather rushed and insane. Malia returned to the sidewalk where her friends were waiting and hoped she wasn't blushing too hard.

They walked in silence for another block, until they were sure it was safe.

"Oh my god," Malia stage-whispered. She thought she might hyperventilate.

"Are you okay?" Dot asked.

"You guys. There is a Veronica concert in two weeks, and Connor is going," Malia practically exploded.

Bree stopped in her tracks. "VERONICA?"

"Clearly we have to go," Malia concluded.

"Veronica?" Bree repeated. "Is coming? Here?" She clutched her chest, like she had just been told something very profound.

"Yes, she's giving a huge concert at the Arts Center," Dot said matter-of-factly. "It was announced weeks ago."

"THE Veronica? In Playa del Mar?" Bree was still trying to make sense of this.

"I think she's incredibly overhyped." Dot sighed. "I mean, I appreciate how she tries to stand for female empowerment, but her songs are very formulaic."

"But you listen to her," said Malia, shooting Dot a look. She knew for a fact that it was true.

"I like to stay up-to-date on popular culture," Dot argued. "I am not, technically, a fan."

"I CAN'T BELIEVE VERONICA IS COMING HERE!" Bree exclaimed.

"Yes, and everyone will be there," Malia added. "Including us."

"We have to go! How much are tickets? How do we buy them? Can we do this now?" Bree spoke, rapid-fire.

"The concert will probably have a decent concession stand," Dot conceded.

"And it will give me so much to talk about with Connor," Malia said wistfully. "Something to really connect over."

"How close do you think we can get? WHAT IF I COULD HUG HER OR EVEN JUST TOUCH HER HAND?" Bree continued to talk at a heightened volume.

"That's exactly how I feel about Connor," Malia said.

"Malia." Bree stopped in her tracks, and grabbed Malia by the shoulders. "We are talking about VERONICA. Like, an actual angel that is coming to our town to grace us with her presence. This is so much bigger than Connor."

"I'll never understand what you see in him," said Dot. "He seems very . . . one-dimensional."

"He doesn't even have any pets," Bree added.

Malia just sighed. Ordinarily, her friends were always on the same page, but when it came to matters of the heart, Malia was used to being on her own. Love was so far beyond reason. It was meant to be experienced, not understood.

First, though, she would have to experience this concert.

Malia didn't care what it took. She would babysit every day —heck, she would babysit every hour—until that concert rolled around. She was going to be there, and it was going to be amazing.

MORE ADVENTURES WITH THE BEST
BAD BABYSITTERS IN THE BUSINESS